"YOU WILL DIE NOW."

The Indian crouched low, knife pointed up. Slocum circled warily. Dodging, he avoided a knife slash intended to bury to the hilt in his belly. He kicked and caught the brave's leg, to no avail. The brave kept his footing and circled, knife flicking back and forth in a deadly curtain of steel.

Slocum lunged forward in full-out attack. He never felt the edge of the knife open a gash along his ribs. Then his arms circled the brave in a powerful bear hug. He lifted and twisted, throwing the man to the ground. Slocum never let loose and followed his opponent down.

Knee coming up, Slocum stunned the Walapai enough to weaken his grip on the knife. Then it was all over. Slocum got his forearm across an exposed neck. Using his full weight, he crushed the life from the warrior . . .

DON'T MISS THESE
ALL-ACTION WESTERN SERIES
FROM THE BERKLEY PUBLISHING GROUP

THE GUNSMITH by J. R. Roberts
Clint Adams was a legend among lawmen, outlaws, and ladies. They called him . . . the Gunsmith.

LONGARM by Tabor Evans
The popular long-running series about U.S. Deputy Marshal Long—his life, his loves, his fight for justice.

SLOCUM by Jake Logan
Today's longest-running action Western. John Slocum rides a deadly trail of hot blood and cold steel.

JAKE LOGAN

SLOCUM AND THE
WALAPAI WAR

J

JOVE BOOKS, NEW YORK

SLOCUM AND THE WALAPAI WAR

A Jove Book / published by arrangement with
the author

PRINTING HISTORY
Jove edition / August 1996

The Putnam Berkley World Wide Web site address is
http://www.berkley.com

ISBN: 0-515-11924-5

A JOVE BOOK®
Jove Books are published by The Berkley Publishing Group,
200 Madison Avenue, New York, New York 10016.
JOVE and the "J" design are trademarks
belonging to Jove Publications, Inc.

PRINTED IN THE UNITED STATES OF AMERICA

10 9 8 7 6 5 4 3 2 1

1

"I'll give you a nickel to beat my dog." The shiny coin glinted in the sunlight as Lieutenant Samuel Gorman held it out to Walapai Charley.

John Slocum pulled down the brim of his dusty black felt hat to shield his green eyes and leaned back in the chair, bracing it against the crumbling adobe wall. Settled and comfortable, he watched the transaction continue between the lieutenant and the old scout.

"Not enough," complained Charley.

"A nickel! You can buy a beer at the post sutler's with it," Gorman said, trying to lure the Indian into doing what he wanted. He held the nickel up so it caught the light and danced it around on Walapai Charley's chest. The Indian looked at the reflection, and Slocum thought he might reach down to try brushing the reflection off his tattered cavalry shirt. But Charley remained stolid. The scout shook his head.

"You drive a hard bargain," said Gorman, warming to the

dickering. "Ten cents. Two nickels."

Slocum saw this had the desired effect. The scout reached out and accepted the pair of coins, then took the short leather strap Gorman wanted him to use on the big yellow dog straining at its leash. The dog barked and whined as if it realized what was in store for it. Slocum guessed the little drama had been played out before.

"Do it hard. Don't stop till I tell you," Gorman called. He sat beside Slocum in front of the camp commander's office.

The mongrel yelped and shied from Charley as the Indian began beating the dog.

"Don't let up now," Gorman said, laughing. He took off his hat, shook dust from the bright gold braid, and dropped it onto his knees. He wiped away sweat, although late March in Arizona was still cool this year. Slocum knew it would get hot quick here just outside Prescott. He had spent too much time farther south in Yuma and Bisbee ever to hanker for that dry, deadly hot desert. The western part of the territory suited him more. The Colorado River flowed fast and cool from the north and winters were almost pleasant, considering some he had weathered in Montana in past years.

"Why do you want Charley to whip your dog like that?" Slocum asked.

Gorman wiped more sweat from his forehead. "It's like this, Slocum. Captain Byrne might be gettin' himself all fired up to sign a treaty with those red devils, but I don't trust 'em. Not a one of 'em."

"Not even Charley? He's scouted against his own people for well nigh two years and never hesitated. He served a year at this post before you transferred in and has never given you reason to doubt his loyalty."

"Can't abide traitors," spat Gorman. "Besides, I've only ridden with him a month. Not time enough to get to know any man, much less a damned redskin." From the storm cloud on the young first lieutenant's fair-skinned face, Slocum figured the officer wasn't likely to cotton to any Indian.

"So?"

"The dog?" Gorman laughed again, more harshly this time. It put Slocum on edge. "That's easy. If the dog is whupped enough by an Indian, he's likely to bark every time one of the savages gets near. That's how I plan to stay alive out here. Old Ulysses is my ears and eyes and nose when I'm asleep."

"The treaty gets the Walapai off their warpath," Slocum said. "Chief Levy-Levy is supposed to be riding in any time now. After that, you won't have any call to be on guard against them."

A touch of melancholy entered Slocum's tone. He had been scouting for Captain Thomas Byrne for over six months. Working for the cavalry at Fort Whipple didn't afford the best pay in the land, but it was a sight better than nothing at all. After the Walapai settled on their government-granted reservation, peace would make his job unnecessary. Experienced officers already found themselves transferred to more active areas of the Western Command, primarily south and east to face the Apaches. Men such as John Slocum wouldn't be required at Fort Whipple much longer.

Slocum considered drifting in that direction to do more scouting for the cavalry, then remembered how hot summer was in the Sonora Desert. It was no better in the Chihuahua Desert snuggling up around Fort Bliss over in Texas.

West. He might ride to the Pacific Coast and head north toward Oregon. Some beautiful country stretched for miles and miles up there, he knew, and the Appaloosas raised in Oregon were to his liking. With luck and a poker game or two along the way, he might have enough to buy a string of the spotted ponies.

"There he comes now," grumbled Gorman. The sandy-haired officer pointed toward the entrance to the camp. Chief

Levy-Levy rode in, surrounded by his counselors. The burly chief looked neither left nor right and dismounted with solemn dignity. He might have been going to his execution rather than to a peace-treaty signing, for all the emotion he showed.

"You have to be at the signing?" Slocum asked.

"Reckon so. The captain ordered it," Gorman said. Louder, he called, "You keep beatin' that dog." With this last order to Walapai Charley, the lieutenant went inside the adobe building, rudely pushing in front of the chief's entourage. Slocum got to his feet and settled his hat. He walked out to where Charley halfheartedly lashed the yellow dog.

"You don't have to do that any more," Slocum said.

"But the lieutenant said—"

"Don't pay him no nevermind," Slocum said. "He's going to be busy for a spell with the peace treaty." Already Slocum heard the formal exchange of greetings. Captain Byrne was a good enough officer, one who refused to show the cruelty Gorman had already. Not that the captain didn't have his problems.

And thinking on one of those personal demons made Slocum's mouth water a mite. It had been too long since he had tasted whiskey. Since this was likely his last day at the post, he might as well ride into Prescott and do some celebrating on his own. Charley might get a beer at the sutler's, but Slocum wanted whiskey.

"If anyone asks, I'm in town wetting my whistle," Slocum said. He brushed off the ever-present dust and walked slowly to his horse. He had ridden patrol this morning, and the horse deserved a rest. Later. Slocum would be sure he found a bag of grain for the steady, sturdy sorrel. Later. After he had quenched his own desert-dry thirst.

Slocum saw no reason to race from Fort Whipple into the town. He rode at a leisurely pace, trying to decide when to leave the service of Captain Byrne and the U.S. Army. With luck, Slocum might be paid until the end of the month. He tried to remember the date and thought it was March 25. He could go on his way with another week's pay if he stayed— if the captain let him stay.

Money was always tight and scouts seemed at the bottom of the list when the paymaster started sliding scrip and coins across the table on payday.

The mile into Prescott went fast for Slocum, as he pondered where he might be traveling soon. The loud cries of cowboys whooping it up told him his choices in saloons. Slocum decided the first saloon he came to was as good as any he was likely to find. He dropped to the ground and tethered his sorrel outside the Dry Gulch Drinking Emporium.

"Whiskey," Slocum said as he settled his elbows on the bar. "Might as well make it a half bottle." The short ride had convinced him his thirst was bigger than he had thought back at Fort Whipple.

"A good choice, John," came a familiar voice.

"Didn't expect to find you here," Slocum said to Daniel Smith. The stolid, weather-beaten translator sat at a table behind him. Slocum snared the bottle of whiskey and dropped beside Smith.

"No need for me to be at the ceremony," Smith said. "The War Department sent out a fancy-ass interpreter to do my job for me."

"Reckon that means you and I are in the same boat. We'll be dismissed sometime tomorrow," Slocum said. He savored the first shot of raw whiskey as it clawed its way down his throat. It pooled warmly in his belly. He had missed this.

"The Warm Springs Apaches are kicking up a fuss again. Don't like San Carlos. General Crook has a way with them and is always on the lookout for good men. Why don't me and you ride that way?"

Slocum made a noncommittal gesture. He had made up his

mind to go west, not south and east to Fort Lowell. But his attention wasn't on the post interpreter but on two miners across the room—and the ravishing redhead seated between them.

Slocum had seen his share of pretty women, but this one had something more than simple beauty. There was a spark of life to her that made him lock his eyes on her trim form and stare rudely. As she turned, her emerald green eyes met his. An almost shy smile crossed her lips, as if she might be embarrassed having Slocum see her in a saloon, then the red-haired belle turned back to her two grizzled miner companions. The three of them rose and left the saloon.

Slocum watched as she left. To his surprise, she paused at the door and glanced over her shoulder at him. Something wasn't quite right, and he finally forced his mind to work on more than her beauty. She wasn't dressed like a dance hall girl. This was no soiled dove plying her trade with horny miners. The redhead was well enough dressed and had an air of dignity to her lacking in loose women. But why was she even in a saloon and with two miners boasting more lust than gold dust?

"She's quite an eyeful, isn't she?"

"What?" Slocum hadn't realized Daniel Smith had been talking, and he had not been listening. "Reckon so." Slocum was not going to discuss her with the post interpreter. For some reason, the redhead drifting across his life for even a few minutes posed a vision too personal to defile by trading lewd fantasies.

"Never saw her in town before," Smith said. When Slocum didn't respond, the interpreter changed the subject. They slowly worked through the half bottle of whiskey. By the time they were down to an inch of amber liquor remaining in the bottom, gunfire brought them up straight in their chairs.

Daniel Smith leaned back and glanced out a dirty window.

"Boys from the post. The treaty must have been signed, and they are coming into Prescott to celebrate."

"I can understand that. No more ambushes, no more patrols and long days in the saddle." Slocum involuntarily ducked as a bullet whined through the open door and blew splinters off the wall over his head.

"The troopers surely are excited," Smith said dryly.

"Looks to be more than the enlisted men," Slocum said when he saw Thomas Byrne swaggering into the saloon. The captain saw his interpreter and scout and came over. His eyes fixed on the almost empty bottle, and he let out a snort of contempt.

"I thought you boys were whiskey drinkers. Let me show you how it's done. Barkeep!" Byrne bellowed. "A bottle! We're celebrating the end of hostilities with the Walapai!"

Byrne took the bottle and upended it. Slocum had seen men swill rotgut before, but never by opening their throat and downing half a bottle without coming up for air. As potent as this tarantula juice was, Byrne might be burning out his throat. He belched at the end of the deep draft and put the bottle on the table.

"Now *that's* the way you drink to celebrate," Byrne said. He belched again and wiped his lips.

"Treaty's all signed, I suppose," said Smith.

"It is, sir. We will finally have some peace," Byrne said.

"Only with Levy-Levy and his band," Smith said. This caused Slocum to sit up a mite straighter and pay attention. Something in the way the interpreter said it carried a touch of danger.

Seeing Slocum's interest, Smith said, "The chief's got a rival still out in the Black Mountains and raising hell."

"Sherum hasn't been much of a problem," Slocum allowed.

"Might be soon, now that Levy-Levy has signed the

treaty," said Smith, warming to the argument. "We might be out on patrol before you know it, Slocum."

"No," cut in Byrne. Slocum sucked in his breath and held it. He knew what was coming. "Fort Whipple's being cut to the bone now that the Walapai are going to their lands to farm."

"Never thought of them as farmers, Captain," said Smith. "They've lived as hunters since they came up from the South."

"They can learn. And we don't need an interpreter much longer. You can stay until the end of the month, Mr. Smith."

Slocum saw the disgust on Daniel Smith's face pass as the captain handed over the bottle. A shot or two of whiskey would be plenty for the interpreter to forget. Not for Slocum. He waited and Byrne finished the dismissal.

"You, Slocum, we don't need any scouts at all. See the paymaster when you get back to the post. He'll have your month's wages. I tried to convince the War Department to give you a bonus for your good work, but—"

"That's all right, Captain," Slocum said. "I know how it is with the military." He had been a captain himself—in the CSA. Slocum had seldom been paid on time or given his full due when Confederate scrip was passed out. But those had been different times.

"I'll buy you another bottle, Slocum. You always were a good sport." Byrne bought a new bottle, but Slocum got precious little of it. Byrne worked steadily on the liquor and surpassed both Smith and Slocum in his thirst. Slocum began to wonder if the cavalry captain was going to be able to stand when they finished.

Somehow, he was only mildly astonished at how unwavering Byrne appeared on his feet. The officer was a hard drinker and knew how to handle his liquor. The trio rose and went to the open saloon door.

"Hate losing good m-men like you," Byrne said. The small stutter was about the only outward sign of his drunkenness. However, Slocum saw how carefully Byrne walked and how the officer kept his hands close to his body. They were shaking like aspen leaves in a high mountain wind.

"Sorry to leave Fort Whipple," Slocum said. "I wanted to—" The thunder of hooves down Prescott's main street was not unusual. The entire while they had been drinking, troopers from the post had hurrahed the town. But after the first round of shots, no more ammunition had been wasted.

Something about the sound of the approaching horses put Slocum on his guard, though. His quick eyes took in the danger, and he shoved Byrne in one direction and crashed into Daniel Smith as he dodged in the other.

A slug whined through the space where Captain Byrne's head had been only an instant before. And it was not the only round making its deadly way in their direction.

Slocum's black felt hat went flying as a slug ripped through the brim. Byrne staggered about, not knowing what was going on. A bullet hit his sword and spun him around—more confused than hurt.

"Get down!" shouted Smith. Slocum watched as if the entire world had been dipped in molasses. A Walapai brave rode up and pointed his rifle at the interpreter. He fired point-blank into Smith's chest. The round shoved Smith backward into Slocum's arms, keeping him from drawing his Colt Navy and returning fire.

"Death to traitors!" cried a war-painted warrior mounted on a fine black stallion. "Death to Levy-Levy!"

With that, the warrior and the braves with him galloped through Prescott, shooting at anyone foolish enough to poke their head outside to see what the commotion was.

"Sherum," muttered Smith. Blood bubbled on his lips.

"We'll get you to a doctor. Don't talk," Slocum said, holding the fallen man.

"Chief Sherum," Smith said, ignoring Slocum. "He's not going to agree to any treaty."

Slocum glanced over at Captain Byrne and saw the officer fumbling to draw his pistol. The threat was long past, but the captain's alcohol-besotted brain still hadn't realized that.

Arizona Territory wasn't going to be as peaceful as anyone had thought just a few hours earlier, Slocum realized. Chief Levy-Levy might have signed a treaty, but Sherum had not.

2

"We've got to get him to a doctor," Slocum said, still cradling Daniel Smith. Blood oozed from the man's mouth, but it wasn't pink and frothy. Sherum's bullet had missed a lung. Still, from the way the wound refused to stop bleeding, Slocum knew the lead had to be removed fast or Smith would die.

When he didn't get any reply from Captain Byrne, Slocum looked up. He saw the cavalry officer wobbling about, trying to hold himself erect. The brief skirmish hadn't unsettled him. Too much booze had. The man was drunker than a lord.

"I'll run 'im into the ground. No Indian's gonna do this to me. Just signed the damn treaty. Can't let Sherum do this, or it'll look real bad," Byrne cried, sitting down hard when his boot heel hit the edge of the boardwalk. He tried to draw his saber, but the single bullet that had come his way had bent the scabbard and prevented it. Giving up on his sword, Byrne worked hard at the flap covering the pistol holstered at his right side.

The weapon proved too much for him to draw. He couldn't even unbutton the leather flap protecting the six-gun. For that Slocum let out a sigh of relief. There was no telling how many—besides himself—Byrne might have shot if he had succeeded.

"A doctor," Slocum said, putting the bark of command into his voice. It had been a spell since he had served as an officer, but the old habit of giving orders came back easily to him. Byrne stiffened, started to salute, and then realized he was being ordered about by a scout. He had the good sense not to argue.

The good sense, Slocum thought, or the haze of liquor tied his brain into knots. Whatever the reason, Thomas Byrne staggered off in search of Prescott's doctor.

"You're not hurt too bad," Slocum said, tugging the fabric of Smith's shirt free. "The wound is cleaning itself, but the bullet has to come out."

"You do it?" Smith's eyelids fluttered. He was fading fast.

"Here comes the town sawbones. Let him have a crack at you. If he doesn't kill you, then I'll try."

Smith smiled weakly.

"Outta the way, youngster. Let me do my job. Them danged Injuns shot more 'n this pup. Got a half-dozen others to patch up 'fore I kin git my dinner." The doctor looked to be a hundred years old, but he opened his bag and drew forth clean instruments. His bony hands were steady, and he seemed confident in what he did. Slocum backed off and watched as the doctor swabbed Smith's wound with alcohol, then inserted a slender steel probe to find the bullet. All the while Captain Byrne shouted orders at his men, who came flocking from all over Prescott.

"Get your mounts, men," Byrne shouted. "We got renegades to find."

"That include me, Captain?" asked Slocum. "You told me
to collect my pay back at the camp."

"That was when we had peace. We have a new war brew-
ing. Damn Sherum! Get your mount, sir. We need you to hunt
them down!" Byrne was no longer slurring his words, but he
continued to wobble about. Slocum nodded, then went to fetch
his sorrel. He had no idea how long the search for Chief
Sherum would last, but it would put a few more dollars into
Slocum's poke.

Slocum knelt and peered along the ground, trying to figure out
how Sherum had hidden the trail so completely. The Walapai
chief had ridden this way. Slocum would have bet a year's
pay on that, but somehow the fleeing Indian chief had successfully covered every trace.

"Well, Slocum, where did those murdering bastards go?"
Lieutenant Gorman stared with such intensity that Slocum
grew uneasy. Gorman acted as if losing the trail was a mark
of incompetence. Or worse.

With skilled men such as Sherum on the run, it came down
to a battle of wits. Slocum was reluctant to admit he was being
outdone.

Standing, Slocum carefully tugged down the brim of his hat
to shield his eyes as he studied the horizon. They had ridden
north from Prescott, heading into rugged country. The first few
attempts Sherum had made to hide his trail were easy for Slocum to discover. Brush pulled behind galloping ponies, dou-
bling back on the trail, other small bits of trail lore had not
confused Slocum.

But now he was at a loss to figure out how Sherum had
simply vanished into thin air. The Walapai might as well have
been a wisp of smoke. Or a ghost.

"The captain wants us to bring them back to stand trial," Gorman said in an icy tone. "It would not do for me to report your failure." The lieutenant bore down on the word "your" to let Slocum know where the sole blame would be placed.

"If you can do a better job, do it," Slocum said in disgust. He turned in a full circle, hoping for a revealing dust cloud or some other sign to put him back on Sherum's trial. He saw nothing, but one branching canyon of towering red rock held his attention. He couldn't say why, but no matter where else he looked, he always came back to stare at the tall, narrow walls of ragged rock leading due west.

"Column, forward!" bellowed Gorman. Slocum started to call to him and then held his tongue. Let the lieutenant blunder about. There was nothing but trouble ahead if Gorman walked into an ambush through his rash actions.

Slocum spat and wiped his lips on his sleeve. He was sore in need of good water, and he hadn't found any during the three-day hunt for Sherum and his braves. Again, the narrow canyon drew his attention. For a moment, he wondered why and then he realized his sorrel was tugging at the reins and edging in that direction.

"Water?" he asked. The horse shook hard, almost pulling Slocum off his feet. He let a bit of the rein slip and gave the horse its head. Walking briskly, he reached the mouth of the canyon in a few minutes. The sorrel wanted to trot now, but Slocum held it back. The horse neighed loudly in protest. Slocum put his hand over the horse's nostrils to quiet it.

The sensation of being watched caused hair to rise on the back of his neck. Slocum always heeded such feelings; they had kept him alive through the war and after. Try as he might, though, Slocum saw no hint that Sherum or anyone else had passed this way recently.

The lofty rock walls gave snipers easy shots at anyone venturing into the canyon. But Slocum saw nothing to show this was a trap. His concentration was broken when his sorrel jerked free and trotted off, making a beeline for a patch of cottonwoods growing a quarter mile away.

Slocum let his horse go. He drew his Colt and followed slowly. Every step made him warier. By the time he reached the small spring where his horse greedily sucked in water, Slocum was ready to explode from tension. Nothing exposed this as a trap, yet every instinct he had honed over the years screamed it.

Dropping to one knee, Slocum scooped up a handful of water and rubbed it over his lips.

"Good water," he said to his horse, still drinking noisily. Slocum dropped onto his belly and thrust his head into the pool, getting trail dust off and only then drinking. Finished, he went to his sorrel and dragged the horse away to keep it from bloating. Only then did he make a careful circuit of the pool, hunting for any trace that Sherum had also watered here.

Nothing.

Sherum had to know every good watering hole in Arizona. That meant Slocum had either completely missed Sherum's trail or the Walapai chief erased every detail of his visit.

A closer second examination of the ground a dozen yards away from the pond turned up hoofprints that had been carefully hidden—maybe. Slocum could not be sure.

"Did we take a wrong turn?" he asked his sorrel. The horse quietly cropped at some blue grama grass growing near the pool and paid him no heed. "Or is this one giant trap?"

To this Slocum had no easy answer. He rested a spell, then decided to rejoin Sam Gorman's column. The troopers and their broken-down mounts could use the water from this spring. Even the Indian-hating lieutenant would not deny that his men needed a rest from their hunt. Slocum spat and considered how he could also make the case for keeping the horses strong so they could pursue Sherum that much longer and harder.

His sorrel complained when he mounted and wheeled about to leave the canyon. Slocum froze.

"Aieee!" came the cry from deeper in the canyon. The echo magnified the sound and sent chills down Slocum's spine. He jerked about and saw a Walapai warrior waving a feathered war lance in the air. With another whoop, the brave put his heels to his pony's flanks and raced into the twisting canyon.

"We've been spotted," Slocum said. He considered his original plan, going for Gorman and returning with the troopers. Then he realized the brave would warn Sherum and either send the Walapai into hiding never to be found or allow time to set up an ambush.

Either way, Slocum thought he could overtake the Walapai scout and stop him from reporting. Spurs raking the sorrel's flanks, Slocum shot off in pursuit. A slow smile crossed his lips when he saw how close to exhaustion the Indian's horse was and how quickly he overtook the escaping brave.

But as he neared, the Walapai turned and stared at Slocum. The expression on his face was not one of fear or determination. It was triumph. A cold knot formed in Slocum's belly. He had been suckered again and was riding headlong into a trap.

Trying to get his horse to stop sent a spray of dust into the air. And Slocum's guess proved all too accurate. The brave didn't ride away, relieved at a sudden reprieve from fighting. The warrior wheeled his own horse and rode straight for Slocum.

A dozen images came to him in a flash. Along the high rim of the canyon sunlight shone off rifle barrels—dozens of rifles, and they guarded the only escape route Slocum had. If he retraced his path he would be filled with several pounds of lead from Walapai rifles.

To either side rose the rugged red rock walls. And ahead? Ahead Slocum saw a half dozen warriors riding to join the one who had lured him so easily into their trap.

"Die!" cried the brave.

Slocum almost fell from the saddle as the brave hurled his lance. The shaft sailed over his head but prevented him from drawing his six-shooter until the Walapai rushed past. Turning in the saddle, Slocum cocked his six-gun and let fly a round. Then another and another. All three missed, and Slocum found himself facing the remainder of the Indians.

If he fought them, he would die quickly. Slocum shuddered. If he fought them he might be captured. Death would not come quickly then.

Letting out a war whoop of his own, Slocum turned his horse and used his spurs to get the horse galloping back down the canyon. He would ride through the gantlet of Sherum's braves on either canyon rim if he kept on, but he hoped their marksmanship was worse than the braves thundering down hard on him from behind.

The brave who had missed him with the lance presented his only barrier to escape—for the moment.

Slocum fired his remaining rounds and finally heard the hammer fall on an empty chamber. Never slackening his pace, he rode down on the Walapai. Swinging his pistol like a club, he struck the warrior on the side of the head and knocked him from his horse.

Escape!

The thought blazed in his brain as he kept his straining horse at full gallop. The sorrel's gait faltered a mite, but Slocum knew he could not give the valiant pony a rest. Not yet. Not when Sherum's men began a barrage from both canyon rims.

Slocum guided his horse toward one towering wall of rock. The braves directly above him had an impossible shot and those on the far side had longer ranges. Not much of an edge, but perhaps enough to keep him alive a few minutes longer. More than his life rode on his escape. He had to get out of the trap to keep Gorman from riding into Sherum's carefully wrought ambuscade.

All the details flowed together in Slocum's head as he dodged the bullets from across the canyon. Some scrub oak gave a moment's respite from the marksmen on the rim, then he found himself confronted with an old threat he had thought long past.

The brave he had buffaloed came running up on foot, knife flashing. With a whoop of triumph, the warrior launched himself and slashed at Slocum. Only by throwing himself out of the saddle did Slocum avoid the deadly blade.

His horse was not as lucky. The gleaming knife cut across the horse's neck, causing a fountain of blood to erupt. The horse reared, kicked out and gave Slocum a few seconds to regain his senses. By the time the sorrel raced away, leaving behind a mist of blood, Slocum had his feet under him and was ready to face the Walapai.

The Indian crouched low, knife point up.

"You will die now," the brave said.

Slocum circled warily. He still presented a good target to the men lining the canyon. When no bullet came singing his way, he knew the gunfire had drawn Gorman and the column of troopers from their path and lured them into the canyon. He had to warn Gorman away or they would be slaughtered.

Slocum realized he had more immediate worries. The brave intended to string his guts from one side of this canyon to another and use them as a clothesline.

Dodging, he avoided a knife slash intended to bury to the hilt in his belly. He kicked and caught the brave's leg, to no avail. The brave kept his footing and circled, knife flicking back and forth in a deadly curtain of steel.

Slocum knew he could attack or he could wait for an opening. If he carried the fight to his opponent he had the best chance of staying alive. The Walapai underestimated him, and in that lay Slocum's only chance. The brave thought he was a coward, intent only on escaping.

Slocum lunged forward in full-out attack. He never felt the edge of the knife open a gash along his ribs. Then his arms circled the brave in a powerful bear hug. He lifted and twisted, throwing the man to the ground. Slocum never let loose and followed his opponent down.

Knee coming up, Slocum stunned the Walapai enough to weaken his grip on the knife. Then it was all over. Slocum got his forearm across an exposed neck. Using his full weight, he crushed the life from the warrior.

Only after the Walapai stopped fighting did Slocum roll away and notice the pain in his side. He groaned as he touched the long, shallow cut across his ribs. The wound wasn't serious, but it bled like a son of a bitch and made movement painful.

A quick grab scooped up the knife that had caused the injury. Slocum tucked it into his gun belt. Then he worked to reload his Colt. Only then did he stumble off in the direction of the canyon mouth. If he didn't get there in time to warn Gorman, the soldiers would be cut to bloody ribbons. They would ride into a canyon lined with Walapai willing to gun them down. Worse, Slocum guessed Sherum's main body of warriors lay deeper in the canyon. The cavalry might ride in, never seeing the trap waiting on the canyon rim. Sherum would launch a frontal assault.

If it succeeded, Gorman's men would be dead. If the soldiers panicked or retreated, the gunfire from the canyon rim would leave no one alive.

Slocum had to keep them away from the canyon and the death waiting inside it.

His stride lengthened as he pressed his shirt against the wound and staunched the bleeding. Strength flowed back when he realized he was not going to die on the spot from either the wound or a new Indian attack. He wished his horse had not run off, but the sorrel might have given him scant speed with the gash across its neck. The only bright spot he saw was the cessation of gunfire from the rim.

Then he realized the sniping at him had stopped because Gorman was riding into the canyon. Sherum would not want to spring the trap too quickly. He wanted to destroy everyone pursuing him. That would be a fitting reply to Chief Levy-Levy's peace treaty.

Passing the watering hole, Slocum found the path he had taken into the canyon and knew he wasn't too far from the mouth of the trap. He alternated running and walking to cover the most distance while maintaining his own strength. Coming out of a stand of palo verde, he saw the glint of sunlight off gold braid. Memories of similar sights returned.

He had been a sniper during the war. Always on the lookout for an officer's gold braid, he would get the man into his sights and rob the soldiers of their commander with the single squeeze of a trigger. Slocum saw that happening again.

He ran forward, waving his arms to draw Gorman's attention.

"Lieutenant!" shouted Slocum. "Gorman! Get back. It's a trap. Get away!"

Slocum shouted until he was hoarse, but Samuel Gorman paid him no heed. Bugle sounding advance, the eager officer led his column of troopers directly into the trap.

3

Slocum hesitated for a moment, then came to a difficult decision. He began shooting at the bugler. He didn't want to injure the man, but if he could draw attention to the danger facing the troopers, the possible wounding or even death of one man meant little.

He missed with every shot. Worse, the bugler never noticed the shots whistling past him. Cursing the distance, Slocum worked to reload. He ran low on ammunition and had only enough for one more full cylinder. The bugler's trumpeting sent the troopers racing into the jaws of a trap they did not even see.

As Slocum began to hope Sherum might have different plans for the cavalry, the trap closed. The warriors on either rim popped up and started firing, driving the soldiers deeper into the canyon. As they galloped forward, their escape was cut off—and they ran headlong into Sherum's main body of braves. The Walapai gave no quarter.

Arrows arced up high into the cloudless Arizona sky and then down into exposed chests. Rifles barked. One after another, the soldiers fell from their mounts. And if the Walapai failed to bring down the troopers, they succeeded in killing the horses under them. Within minutes, a battered remnant of Gorman's command huddled in a grove of acacia, with no way to escape save on foot.

Slocum hesitated. He was a hundred yards away from where the lieutenant had made his stand against Chief Sherum. If Slocum joined the troopers, he would die with them. Away, he might get help.

Slocum snorted. He knew better than to ever consider that. Captain Byrne had been drunker than a lord when he sent them from Prescott in search of Sherum. Since then, any number of things might have happened and none of them good. Slocum had no way of knowing if another cavalry column rode within twenty miles of them.

And then the matter was taken from his hands. Bullets kicked up tiny puffs of dust behind him, forcing him into the middle of the canyon and exposing him to fire from both rims. Try as he might, he could not find the hidden rifleman driving him toward the grove as he might herd stray cattle.

"Slocum, get down!" bellowed Gorman. "Don't come in here. Go for help!"

Slocum wished that were possible. He winced and fell face-down in the dirt as a bullet skipped along his shoulder blades. Crawling, he found temporary refuge behind a fallen log. Splinters erupted from this hiding spot as the Walapai sniper sighted in on him. Slocum saw he had no chance of getting out of the canyon and the trap Sherum had sprung so expertly. Anywhere he might run was exposed. Worse, the hidden rifleman who had driven him to this spot was still a factor. As he lifted his head, a bullet ripped through the crown of his black felt hat.

Feinting to the right, Slocum rolled left and avoided a new fusillade of bullets. Feet kicking up a dust cloud, he sprinted for the dubious safety of the acacia. All that saved him was ragged supporting fire from the troopers.

He doubted Lieutenant Gorman had ordered it. The troopers had acted on their own.

"Cease firing, don't waste your ammo," shouted Gorman. "Dammit, he was supposed to get help, not join us. Cease fire! Sergeant Donnelly, get your men under cover and stop wasting ammo!"

Slocum sat up, his back to a low, ragged-barked tree. He moaned as he rubbed the fresh wound against the acacia's roughness.

"Thanks," he said to Sergeant Andrew Donnelly and two privates. They had disobeyed Gorman's orders and had saved his hide.

"Why'd you let us ride into the trap, Slocum?" Gorman demanded. "You were supposed to scout for us, not get us into trouble like this. They'll have our scalps before sundown!"

"Don't think so," Slocum said.

"What? Why not?"

"They'll lift our hair within the hour unless you have more ammunition than I think you do," Slocum said, getting to his feet. His body ached and the white-hot lance of pain in his side and shoulders fogged his mind. But Slocum knew he had to fight if they were going to win free.

"What are we gonna do, Lieutenant?" asked Donnelly, a swarthy veteran of too many Indian skirmishes. "They shot up our horses. Not a one of them nags is livin'."

"And," cut in a young private, a catch in his voice, "they shot up better 'n half our company. They got Pete. I kin see him out there in the sun."

Slocum reached out and grabbed the boy's wrist to keep

him from lifting his rifle and taking a shot at the buzzard hopping awkwardly along the ground to eat the fallen trooper.

"Save your bullet," Slocum warned.

"You're right, Slocum," the boy said. "I'd feel a dang sight better if I got one of them red niggers. Pete'd appreciate that." The private yanked away and stalked to a post at the far side of the grove. Slocum knew calling Sherum and his braves names wasn't going to improve their condition any, and it might even cloud judgment when a clear head was needed.

"Can we hold out until sundown?" asked Gorman. The lieutenant paced like a caged animal.

"Don't count on it," Slocum said. He eyed the tall cliffs on either side and knew the Walapai along the rims had an easy shot at anyone leaving the copse. Worse, he felt Sherum's other braves working their way toward them. The Walapai would massacre them in minutes.

"Got a lucifer?" Slocum asked suddenly.

"What? Yes, here. You hankering for one last smoke?" Gorman fumbled out a metal cylinder holding the matches.

"Get ready to run for the far side of the canyon," Slocum said. "I'm going to create a little diversion. Get your men ready, Donnelly, Framingham, Proctor."

"Wait, you can't do that. We need these trees for cover!" protested Gorman when he saw what was about to happen. But Slocum had already ignited the dried leaves at their feet. Fallen branches crackled and popped and sent tongues of flame leaping upward. Green leaves still clinging to tree limbs smoldered and sent billows of dark, greasy smoke into the air. In less than a minute the tiny grove was a raging inferno—and the canyon was filled with obscuring haze.

"Go, run!" Slocum shouted at the noncoms. "Get to the north wall. We can make a better stand there." He heard Gorman trying to regain command of his men and failing. The soldiers coughed and gagged on the smoke. This drove them into the open, but the very fire causing them to run protected them from the Walapai.

For a few minutes.

"Now what?" asked Gorman, wiping soot from his eyes as he pressed against the rocky canyon wall. Others joined them, panting harshly from their desperate sprint.

"We're protected from the snipers above us," Slocum said. "And we know they can't sneak up on us from behind."

"They're dropping rocks!"

Slocum threw up his arm to protect his face as a boulder crashed into the ground a few feet away. He had been right that the Walapai could no longer shoot at them from one rim. He had neglected to consider they might push rocks over the edge onto their heads.

"You're going to get us killed, Slocum. You have any more harebrained schemes?"

"Write me up and put me on report when we get back to Fort Whipple," Slocum said sarcastically. He clutched his six-shooter and chanced a glance upward. If he had failed to hit the bugler on his charge of fifty yards, he had no chance at all of an upward shot at a dodging Walapai warrior at twice the range.

"They're movin' in on us again," warned Sergeant Donnelly. "What do we do, Slocum?"

"We fight," Gorman said, giving Slocum an angry look. "I am in command, and you will obey *my* orders, Sergeant."

The enlisted man looked from Slocum to Gorman and back. Slocum inclined his head, indicating the sergeant ought to obey his commanding officer. Gorman had as good a chance of getting them away safely as Slocum did—it required the same miracle, no matter who gave the orders.

On Gorman's order, the soldiers began firing measured volleys into the advancing Walapai. Slocum held his own fire, waiting for a clear target. Sherum's braves were too cagey for that. They used the sparse shelter of rock and brush well as they advanced. One by one, Gorman's men fell, either to arrow or rock tumbling from above.

"I cain't take this no longer!" screamed the boy whose friend had been killed. The private jumped to his feet and charged. His carbine jammed, but he never noticed. He ran forward, swinging the rifle as if it were a club.

Slocum tried to give covering fire, hoping the boy would come to his senses. The young private died with an arrow in his chest before that happened.

"Damnation," muttered Gorman. "They got us now."

"Something's wrong," Slocum said, twisting around and listening intently. "They've stopped the attack. Why would they do that? A single rush would exhaust our ammunition. They have to know we have only a few rounds left."

"Who knows what's in their heads?" grumbled Gorman.

"Bugler!" called Slocum. "Start tooting on that noise-maker of yours. Make all the noise you can!"

"Why?" asked Gorman. "What's—"

"Do it!" Slocum fired the remaining rounds in his six-shooter as the bugler pulled the instrument to his lips and started playing the mournful "Dan Butterfield Blues." Slocum thought it appropriate—and yet they might not be buried this day.

"Lieutenant, there. In the mouth of the canyon. I see a pennant! It's Captain Byrne! We're saved!" The bugler made the mistake of standing and waving frantically at his commanding officer. He never heard the sharp crack of the rifle firing at him. The round caught him smack in the head, and he fell to the ground, dead before he touched dirt.

"Keep trumpeting, somebody," Gorman ordered, "and the rest of you, keep your danged heads down or you'll get them blown off like the bugler just did."

Slocum pushed his back against the cold rock and watched as Byrne charged into the flank of Sherum's fighters. The Walapai on the rim fired halfheartedly, then vanished from sight. Those on the canyon floor quickly disappeared, also, smoke on the wind. Slocum didn't care much for any cavalry officer at the moment, but he was glad to see Byrne ride up.

"Lieutenant, get what's left of your men back to Fort Whipple," Byrne ordered upon reining back a few yards away. "We will need all the trained soldiers we can muster if we are to carry this war to Sherum."

"Sir," Gorman said, glaring at Slocum. "I want to report the loss of most of my men. Slocum led us into a trap. He—"

"Have your men ride double, Lieutenant," Byrne said, as if not hearing his subordinate. Slocum saw the captain's bloodshot eyes and the way he wobbled in the saddle. Byrne had been drinking heavily—constantly—and this kept him from understanding Gorman's accusations.

Slocum wasn't sure if this was a good thing or not. Sherum was too wily an opponent for Byrne not to stay cold sober in the field. It might be for the best if he used some of the pay he had been accumulating, bought a new horse, and simply rode off to Oregon as he had planned.

Still, as he swung behind a corporal and looked out over the scene of the ambush, Slocum knew he would not do that. This fight with the Walapai chief was taking on the air of a personal affront. Sherum had bested him on the trail and killed a good horse, not to mention making him look foolish in the eyes of the soldiers. Slocum wasn't sure which was the worst.

And it did not matter. He wasn't going to run from this fight. Not if Byrne kept him on as scout.

"You will do anything to get out of a passel of work, won't you?" Slocum joshed Daniel Smith. The interpreter lay propped up in the bed at the rear of the doctor's office. Pale but alert, Smith nodded.

"Heard the orders. Can't say they make much sense to me, but if it means I miss moving Fort Whipple to a new camp, fine. The food's better here than the cook ever served."

"There's some logic to the move," Slocum said. "Whipple isn't serving any purpose now that Sherum is on the warpath. By building a new stockade at Beale Springs, we can cut off an important watering hole."

"Beale Springs? Don't know it," said Smith. He shifted in the bed, getting his bandaged arm settled.

"It's between here and Fort Mojave," Slocum said. "The War Department thinks it is a good move."

"You don't, do you, John?"

Slocum shook his head. He had seen how easily Sherum found water in the mountains north of Prescott. Beale Springs was an important source of water for the white man, but not necessarily for the Walapai.

"There's no more talk of cutting back on the garrison," Smith went on, seeing Slocum's answer in his grim expression. "We got jobs again."

"You heal up. I have to scout the road to be sure Sherum doesn't ambush us again. There's hardly half the men left in the garrison after our foray north."

"Watch your back, John. And I don't mean from just Sherum and his braves."

Slocum nodded. Although bedridden, Smith had heard of Sam Gorman's growing animosity. But this wasn't the first time Slocum had dealt with men who didn't cotton much to him. He had a job to do, and he would do it better than before now that he realized how dangerous Chief Sherum was.

Stepping onto Prescott's main street, Slocum took a deep breath of hot, dusty air. It was hard to believe it was getting into April already. As he looked around, his eyes lit upon the trim figure of a redhead. For a moment, he struggled to re-member where he had seen her. Then it came to him.

She had been in the saloon the day Sherum shot up the town. Slocum had not gotten a good look at her then. He did now. She hurried across the street, her bustle waggling seductively. The dry spring wind caught her fine hair and carried it away from her pale oval face like a coppery banner. Then she disappeared into a dress shop.

Slocum heaved a sigh. It would be a long time before he saw a lady as lovely as that one again. He had a long scout ahead of him, one filled with blood and death. Swinging onto the bay he had spent fifty dollars to buy from the town ostler, he rode from Prescott heading directly for Beale Springs two hours away.

4

It had been a hard week, and Slocum ached all over. He stretched his tired muscles as he studied the new camp. Alongside the men of Captain Byrne's severely diminished command, Slocum had worked long hours to get trees cut and adobe bricks made for a dozen buildings near the spring bubbling up from the ground. The new post now commanded all routes leading to Beale Springs and could deny Sherum water.

Slocum doubted that would be enough to stop the rampaging Walapai chief. Reports had come in all week long of miners being killed in the hills. Byrne had grown tired of responding to such claims, deciding his first duty lay in constructing the post. If half the reports were accurate, Sherum had killed more than a dozen men since ambushing Gorman's company.

"Good work," Byrne said, coming from his quarters in the new small adobe house near the parade grounds. "Good work, yes, you have done well." He dispensed his benediction as he crossed to the low wood rail fence circling the camp.

From the way he walked, Byrne had been sampling his private stock of Old Overholt. Slocum vowed not to light a match too close to the captain. Otherwise, the entire camp might go up in a bright blue flame as the whiskey fumes ignited.

"Slocum, a word with you." Captain Byrne motioned him over. Slocum brushed his hands on his jeans and went to see what was on the officer's whiskey-blurred mind. Byrne propped himself against a hitching post and waited for Slocum to stop in front of him.

"I have a mission for you, sir. Sherum is raiding unchecked, and I need to know his strengths. How many men does he command, how are they armed, do they have adequate horses and supplies, that sort of thing."

"Sounds like you want me to fight the whole war," Slocum said. "If I could get that close to Sherum, I could take him prisoner and bring him back for trial."

"Your attitude leaves much to be desired, Slocum. Lieutenant Gorman told me of your failure on the scout and how it cost him much of his command, but I had not believed him. You were always a good scout. Are you turning soft toward the Walapai?"

Slocum wondered if the liquor was doing the talking or if Byrne meant what he said.

"Captain, any time you're not satisfied with me or my work, pay me my due and I'll ride out of here."

"Captain," spoke up the corporal who had been working alongside Slocum all day. "There's no need to worry about him. He's been doin' the work of two men. We're so short-handed right now, we could use a dozen more like him."

"When I want your opinion, I shall ask for it, Corporal Framingham." Byrne glared at the enlisted man and backed him down. The corporal turned and went off, muttering to himself, leaving Byrne to vent his spleen on Slocum.

"Now, Slocum, are you refusing this mission?"

"Gets me out of doing more carpentry work," Slocum allowed. "When do you want me on the trail?"

"Right away. I—" Captain Byrne paused when the sentry posted at the west end of the fort waved to attract attention. "One moment. There seems to be a disturbance of some kind." Byrne strode off. Slocum followed at a distance. He made a slight detour to his open-air bivouac, retrieved his gun belt and six-shooter and strapped them on before joining Byrne.

The man who had stumbled into camp looked like buzzard bait. Blood caked his arms and body, and he might have eaten something more substantial than insects during the past week, but Slocum doubted it from the look of his scrawny frame. From the canvas britches and the filthy shirt—what showed of it through the blood—the man worked as a miner.

"Injuns," the skeletal miner grated out. He took a few faltering steps forward and collapsed. Byrne started to catch him, then considered how filthy the man was and stepped away at the last moment. He let the miner tumble facedown into the dirt at his feet.

"Get the doctor," Byrne ordered. He punctuated the order with a grand sweeping arm motion that almost threw him to the ground beside the miner. Byrne recovered his balance and glared at the ring of soldiers, daring them to make any mention of his drunkenness. Not a trooper faced their commander squarely.

Slocum pushed through the small knot of soldiers and rolled the miner onto his back.

Watery blue eyes flickered open and fixed on Slocum. A gnarled hand reached out and grabbed Slocum's shirt to keep him from leaving.

"Mule died on me a few miles down the road. Ole Bessie June was a good mule. Had her for years."

"What happened to you?" Slocum asked. Mules died. So did men, but it was the cavalry's duty to find out why.

"Walapai. They came swoopin' into our camp. Never had a chance. Monty had an old black powder Remington. Hadn't loaded it in years. No good. No balls for it. Captured 'em, both of 'em. Monty and his sister."

"What do you mean, 'his sister'?" Slocum shook the miner to focus his attention. Wiping some of the grime away revealed a face Slocum remembered. He had been one of the two miners with the lovely redhead on their arms back in Prescott, just after Chief Levy-Levy signed the peace treaty at Fort Whipple.

"Moira's her name. Them Injuns took Monty and her. Six days ago. Couldn't stop 'em. Too many."

"Was it Sherum's band?" asked Captain Byrne.

"Sherum? Didn't ask his name." The miner shuddered and coughed. Slocum rolled him onto his side to keep his windpipe clear. The miner hawked up a bloody gob.

"Make way, can't get to him if you don't let me through." The post physician dropped beside the miner. Slocum wondered if Doc Gavilan had been drinking with Byrne. The bloodshot eyes were a clue, but the liquor on his breath was enough to knock over a plow horse. He couldn't help comparing the post doctor with the one in Prescott.

If the miner was lucky enough and tough enough, he would live to reach Prescott and decent medical care.

"I recognize him," said Corporal Framingham, who had come to Slocum's defense earlier. "He's got a silver mine and—"

"You know where it is?" interrupted Slocum.

"More or less. Never been there, but I can find it."

"Slocum, get out there. Corporal, select ten troopers and accompany him."

"Right away, sir." Framingham held back his broad grin

until he turned from his commander. Being in the saddle, even the uncomfortable McClellan saddle, was an improvement over making mud bricks and building corral fences.

Slocum left the doctor working on the miner and went to saddle his bay gelding. He cared less about leaving behind the camp at Beale Springs than he did about finding the red-haired woman he had seen in Prescott. He knew what happened to women taken prisoner by the Indians. Campfire tales about the Oatman girls taken by the Apaches down around Yuma came back to haunt him.

That was no fate for any woman, much less one as lovely as the one he had seen in Prescott.

"How on earth did the miner ever make it to Beale Springs so quick?" Slocum wondered aloud. The terrain had grown increasingly steep the past day. The miner's mule must have had wings on its hooves to cover the distance so quickly.

"They know every turn and canyon in the hills," Framingham said. "He might have taken a shortcut getting to the post." The corporal rose in the stirrups and carefully studied the rocky terrain around them, hunting for any sign of Sherum and his warriors. Slocum knew that any trace discovered would mean Sherum was luring them into a trap. The Walapai chief was too good a trailsman to leave behind signs useful in tracking him.

"There's a sign," Slocum said. He rode forward and jumped from his horse. He picked up the battered wooden sign and brushed off dirt. "The Three Card Monte."

"Must be the one. Heard him call his partner Monty." The corporal got his troopers in a single-file line and spaced them at uneven intervals to keep any possible ambush from killing more than a few. Slocum was pleased with Framingham's savvy.

Slocum rode ahead, wary of every shadow and jumping at

each quail or dove he flushed from cover. He had never encountered an enemy quite as expert as Sherum before, and it put him on edge.

Reining back after several hours of arduous riding, Slocum held up his hand. They had followed the narrow road for almost ten miles without a sign of Walapai until he saw a broken arrow in the road. As he more carefully studied the area, other traces leaped out at him, almost screaming after the lack of evidence to this point.

A bit of torn leather, an eagle feather, partial moccasin prints—and shell casings—all told the story of the attack. Slocum circled the area, finally giving up on Walapai sign. There was too much. He climbed to the top of a large boulder and lay flat. His sharp eyes worked over the twenty yards leading to a ramshackle line cabin.

No sign of life. No hint of motion. Not even a whisper of wind to relieve the utter silence. Slocum hoped it wasn't the silence of the grave he listened to so intently. They had ridden hard to get here—and Sherum's attack had taken place almost two weeks earlier.

He rolled over and waved off Corporal Framingham. The soldier nodded and returned to his squad to keep them in check. Slocum appreciated such competence. It was rare in any trooper at Beale Springs. Too many joined their commander in an alcoholic haze or outright, mind-numbing hatred like that chewing at Gorman's gut.

Sliding like a snake, Slocum worked closer to the cabin. A dark patch in the dry earth caught his attention. He touched the caked dirt and knew the mud had been made with blood. Lots of blood.

The miner making his way back to the cavalry post had bled profusely. This might be his. Or it could be his partner's—or Moira's. Slocum tried to shake off the dread he felt at the notion of the woman's death. He had never met her. He had seen her for less than a minute on two separate occasions, but her beauty haunted him. It was a damned shame any woman had to come to the West and die. For some reason, he felt the loss even more with Moira.

Slocum drew his six-shooter and spun, ready to shoot anyone inside the cabin. The faint light filtering inside revealed only three thin pallets. Empty. Two chairs at a lopsided table. Empty. The entire cabin was vacant with no sign that life had existed here any time during the past week.

A grating sound behind him sent Slocum whipping around and into a gunfighter's crouch.

"Whoa, Slocum, it's me. The men ringed the area and found nothing." Corporal Framingham held his carbine at his side, not ready for any ambush Sherum might spring.

"You're sure the place is deserted?"

"As empty as a two-bit whore's promise," Framingham said.

"I want to see if the miner and his sister holed up in the mine."

"I'd be mighty careful doin' that, Slocum," said Framingham, looking uneasy. "That mine's not got a single good timber in it. The roof might fall in on your head."

"It won't take long."

Slocum paused at the mouth of the mine shaft. From only a quick glance the corporal had given a good description of the shoring in the Three Card Monte. Most of the decent trees nearby had been cut by earlier miners for their empty rock pits or burned for firewood to protect against the Arizona winter.

Hand against one bent timber, Slocum took a tentative step forward. The timber moaned in protest that anyone other than the mine owners had entered. He found a half dozen miners' candles high on a shelf. He lit one, cradled the flame, and went a bit deeper into the mine.

"Slocum!" came the call from outside.

"What? You find them?"

"Them? You mean the Walapai or the miner and his sister?" asked the corporal.

"Either, both." Slocum held his irritation in check. Being in the dusty mine put his nerves on edge.

"No sign of any of 'em."

Slocum turned and retreated, both glad to be out of the low-roofed shaft and annoyed because he wanted to be certain Moira and her brother hadn't taken refuge here against the Walapai. If anything had happened to them, they might need his help getting free.

Bright sunlight caused him to squint. Framingham and the rest of the squad were spread out around the camp. Some leaned on their rifles, others were building smokes.

"That smart?" Slocum said, indicating the soldiers smoking.

"The Walapai are long gone. So's the miner. We're heading back to the camp."

"You enjoy making mud bricks that much?" asked Slocum. From the expression on Corporal Framingham's face, he knew the patrol would take the long way back. They had no desire to rejoin the construction at Beale Springs and even less to engage Chief Sherum's warriors.

"There's nothing more we can do here. We ought to report to the captain."

Slocum was torn between returning with the patrol and continuing his search. He had found no sign of the miner and his sister but had no reason to doubt the man who had struggled to reach the cavalry and beg for help.

"Go on. I'll poke around and see if I can find the Walapais' trail," Slocum said. The corporal shook his head at such diligence, then formed his men and rode out single file. Slocum watched them go, wondering if he'd made a mistake continuing the hunt. He shook his head, turned and went back into the mine shaft to ferret out any clue to the whereabouts of the miner.

And his sister.

5

Slocum burst into the sunlight, gasping for air. The mine had pockets of gas that had almost overwhelmed him. Sinking to his heels, he leaned against the side of the sheer mountain. He had worked around mines enough to know this was a worthless hole in the rock. Not enough silver was left to make even a silver dollar.

Worse, he had found no trace of Monty or his sister. Evidence of two men working in the mine lay at every turn in the well-picked shaft, but nothing showed any woman had entered the mine. That didn't surprise him too much. Most miners were superstitious and would never allow a woman to jinx their claim by entering.

Still, he refused to believe the miner struggling into Beale Springs had lied. Why was there no sign of a struggle other than the few feathers and bits of leather left by the Walapai—and the dirt where someone had bled profusely?

It was as if the site had been swept clean to prevent any pursuit.

"Almost as if Sherum's camp were nearby and he didn't want people nosing around," Slocum said softly to himself. The Walapai chief had shown himself to be cautious when required and bold if the opportunity for a trap presented itself. Which side of the Walapai chief's personality was revealed most in his raid on this mining camp?

Slocum heaved himself erect and made a more careful study of the cabin and the parched ground around it. He found more blood spots in the dirt, but these were drops, not the gusher that had caused the dirt-and-blood patch farther down the hillside. Heading along a faint game trail in the direction indicated by the blood, Slocum froze in his tracks when he saw the first real clue.

Reaching out, he pulled a bit of yellow cloth from a thorny pad of a prickly pear cactus. No matter Monty's taste in clothing, he wasn't likely to wear yellow-dyed cotton. Slocum dropped to the ground and made a more careful study. He found scuff marks against the rocks and even more certain indication of Walapai passing by recently in a few turquoise beads that had popped off a necklace and fallen into the cactus patch.

Was it a trap or had Sherum figured no one would be as persistent as Slocum to track this far from the mine? Opting for caution, Slocum left the game trail where he had found the scrap of fabric and beads. He worked his way higher on the steep mountainside until he was gasping for breath. Even though he rested frequently, the way proved increasingly harder, spines catching at his clothing and the tangled undergrowth almost impassable in places. Slocum moved as quietly as he could—and thanked his lucky stars for this seemingly irrational vigilance.

A hundred feet below him, on either side of the game trail,

he saw four Walapai braves patiently standing guard. Two rested on their rifles. The other pair was armed with bows and arrows. He might have blundered along the lower path and fallen into a trap if he had not decided to travel the more difficult route higher on the mountain.

Slocum considered removing the braves one by one and knew that was a fool's quest. Sherum camped nearby, which was the reason he had attacked the miners at the Three Card Monte. The chief didn't want to be found by the cavalry. Slocum had to be sure Sherum didn't know his raid on the mine had created the very situation he wanted to avoid until it was too late.

The day faded quietly, shadows lengthening as Slocum sat and watched the four Indians below him. Others came and took their place as sentries just after sundown. When they did, Slocum softly padded along a parallel course, following them to their camp a mile distant. Like their Apache brothers, the Walapai did not camp at their watering hole. Rather, they remained a hundred yards distant so small game would continue to drink undisturbed.

And with that drinking came death. Slocum watched as two Walapai bagged a half-dozen rabbits and a small deer, enough to feed a good-sized war party. He trailed the hunters to the edge of their camp, where other small animals roasting filled the air with a nose-tingling fragrance.

But the small cooking fires held his attention more than what roasted there. Dozens of warriors gathered, all heating their knives. Slocum went cold inside when he realized why they were doing this. His eyes moved from the red-hot blades to the man staked out in the center of the camp.

They were torturing the miner. Of his sister Slocum saw no trace, but she had to be near unless she had already died.

Screams rent the air as the hot knives sliced through Monty's flesh.

"You bastards. Won't tell you nuthin'." He groaned as new tortures were meted out. "Don't have nuthin' to tell. But if I did, I'd lie!"

Slocum admired the man's courage if not his good sense. If Monty had nothing to say, he ought to have lied. His tongue ought to have been flapping like a flag in the wind. As it was, all Slocum saw ahead for the man was painful death. For whatever reason, the torture had begun recently and not two weeks earlier when the miner had been captured at the mine. No one survived weeks of this agony. No one.

"Stop! Don't do this to him. He can't tell you a thing," came a woman's frantic voice. Moira fought to get free of rawhide thongs binding her to an oak a few yards away. She sat in shadow, and Slocum had missed her because of his intent study of the miner and his tormenters.

As Moira leaned forward, the light from the campfires caught her hair and turned it from copper to pure spun gold. He had never seen a woman so lovely—or so hysterical.

"Stop it, don't hurt him, he knows nothing," she shouted over and over. From the expressions on the Walapai braves' faces, they enjoyed her agitation more than they did torturing her brother. Slocum's fingers curled around the ebony butt of his Colt as he thought of what else the Walapai might enjoy later.

After Monty was dead.

Slocum vowed to save the woman or, if he could not do that, then kill her. Leaving her to the captivity and degradation promised by the renegades tore at his belly like a gaping wound.

Moving like a shadow through other shadows, Slocum circled the camp and came up behind Moira. She had subsided, sitting cross-legged on the ground, a rawhide thong binding her tightly. Tears flowed down her cheeks, leaving muddy tracks. She stared at her brother, who had stopped complaining minutes before Slocum got into position.

The miner had died in anguish. How long before the Walapai turned their attention to their female captive?

Slocum wasn't sure, but one thing was certain. He had damned little time to free Moira—and he had no idea at all how they were going to escape on foot. He had left his horse back at the Three Card Monte mine, a couple miles off. If Corporal Framingham had not rushed away, Slocum might have had a ghost of a chance in this rescue. But even with the cavalry to support them, it would be well nigh impossible to get free. They had to travel rugged mountain paths in the dark, with a pack of snapping Walapai renegades on their heels.

The only luck he was likely to get came when Sherum stood and motioned for his braves to join him at the largest bonfire in the middle of camp. This huge fire showed the Walapai's contempt for cavalry pursuit. Either that or his scouts assured him the bluecoats were back at Beale Springs and posed no threat.

"Moira," Slocum called. "Back of you. Here, in the shadows."

"What? Who are you? How do you know my name?" The fiery redhead spun about, straining at the rawhide holding her so securely. "Are you here to rescue us?"

"I am if you'll keep your voice down." Slocum jerked his thumb in the direction of Chief Sherum, strutting about and haranguing his war party. Slocum didn't understand much of the Walapai tongue, but he knew the chief was working up the braves, telling them something about never settling along the Colorado River. That part Slocum didn't know or care about. He had to free the woman.

Like a snake, he slithered close enough to slide a knife blade back and forth on Moira's bonds. They snapped free. She gasped with relief and began rubbing circulation back into her hands. Slocum worked even harder on the thong holding her to a stake.

"You're free. Move slowly and come back into the darkness. I don't know how we are going to get away but—"

"What?" Moira sat bolt upright and stared at him. Bright green eyes blazed with fury. "You're not rescuing just *me*. You've got to save Montgomery, also! They are doing terrible things to him. You can't *leave* him!"

"Hush," Slocum said, trying to silence her. The Walapai paid attention to their chief, but the spell was fading as the warriors thought again of Moira. All it would take for the rescue to turn to disaster was one brave glancing over.

"I will not," she said, ire rising. "He is my brother, and I will not abandon him to these savages!"

"These savages will have their way with you if you don't save yourself," Slocum said.

"You're the one doing the rescuing. So do it! And do not neglect my brother," she said, arms crossed over her ample breasts.

From the set to her firm chin, Slocum knew argument would not work. He scooted closer. A small smile came to her lips.

"I knew you would see it my w—" She never finished. Slocum cocked back his fist and slugged her. Her head snapped back, and she sagged to the ground, unconscious.

For an instant, Slocum feared the furious activity had alerted the Indians. He relaxed when he saw that they had begun dancing about the fire, whooping and goading each other to tell tall tales of their conquests.

Slocum reached out and grabbed a handful of the dirty yellow dress Moira wore. He began dragging her away, wondering what he was going to do once he got her out of sight. If she remained senseless, he could never hope to carry her to safety, but awake she might start a ruckus that would bring the Walapai down on them.

He saw no way out but to try. Lugging her through the underbrush caused noise loud enough to awaken the dead. Slocum stopped after less than ten yards, knowing he would never be able to get Moira to freedom. Thinking he might steal a pair of ponies, he left her propped against a juniper and went to test his horse-thieving skills. It took less than a minute for him to realize Lady Luck had abandoned him entirely.

The horses were on the far side of the camp, and he saw no fewer than three guards posted to prevent theft. They paid little attention to the horses, but the animals were straining against their hobbles. If Slocum so much as walked in their direction they would let out loud neighs that would draw unwanted attention.

He pushed the notion of stealing horses from his mind and kept moving. His toe cracked against something hard in the darkness, sending him pitching forward. He caught himself in time to keep from making any more noise. The dancing, chanting Indians had not heard him.

Fumbling about, Slocum ran his fingers over the box he had so clumsily encountered. He traced out the rough dimensions of a crate. Wishing for more light but knowing he dared not hold up anything he found for fear of discovery, he had to guess at what he had found.

A slow smile curled his lips. The Walapai had looted everything of value from the Three Card Monte Mine—and that included a box of dynamite, complete with blasting caps and miner's black fuse. Slocum scooped up what he could from the wooden crate and crept back to where Moira stirred.

She moaned and rubbed her jaw.

"You hit me," she mumbled.

"I'll do it again if you don't keep your tater trap shut," Slocum said. He worked quickly to roll tape around sticks of dynamite. He bit down hard on the blasting cap to crimp it, then thrust the fuse in the middle of the bundle.

"That's no way to treat a lady," she said, gingerly pressing her fingers into the injured jaw. "And you didn't tell me how you knew my name."

"Your brother's partner made it to the cavalry post at Beale Springs. He kept calling your name over and over. Moira."

"Moira Kelson," she said. "And that's my brother Montgomery Kelson those savages have tied to the ground and are torturing. They have left us alone for weeks while they were out raiding. Only this evening did they return. Their chief saved us for this celebration over who knows what."

"Miss Kelson," Slocum said, trying to find the right way of telling her they had to escape and that her brother was likely dead, "there's nothing we can do for Monty."

"Monty," she said, her face showing a hint of animation. "Only Sean calls him that. His partner, the one back at your camp." She eyed Slocum, as if for the first time. "You don't have the look of a military man about you, now do you?"

"I'm a scout," Slocum said. "There's a column of troopers back at the mine," he lied. "We can get to them, and they'll be here in jig time to rescue your—"

"No! We do it *now*," she said with grim determination. "I read it in your face. You're wantin' to leave him here, now aren't you?"

"Miss Kelson," Slocum said in exasperation. "Moira. He's dead. They tortured him to death!"

"He is not!" she exclaimed, shooting to her feet. "He is too tough to ever succumb."

"Shut up," Slocum said, but he saw it was too late. Whether a guard had noticed their prisoner was missing or Moira's outburst had alerted Sherum, he would never know. The dancing stopped and all eyes turned in their direction.

"Draw your weapon. Shoot them. And save Montgomery."

Slocum pushed her aside and stood. He faced dozens of Walapai renegades, warriors rebelling against not only Chief

Levy-Levy but the U.S. Government. Six shots would do nothing but arouse them, anger them enough to keep him alive for long, agonizing days instead of killing him quickly as they had Montgomery Kelson.

"Stay behind me," Slocum said. Not waiting to see if she obeyed, he fumbled in his vest pocket and found his lucifers. He drew one, struck it and lit the black fuse. It sizzled, popped, and began spitting sparks into the night.

Slocum clutched the bundle of dynamite and held it in front of him as he marched into the circle of light cast by the Walapais' bonfire. All eyes were fixed on him and the dynamite he held at arm's length so everyone could see it. The only sound as he walked was the crackling of the juniper-fed campfire and the hissing fuse.

6

Slocum held the dynamite bundle at arm's length as he walked close enough for the Indians to see the black fuse. It sparkled and sputtered like Fourth of July fireworks as he thrust the deadly packet high above his head.

The reaction was everything Slocum had hoped for. The Walapai let out yelps of terror and scattered into the darkness.

They all ran except Sherum. The Walapai chief stood and stared at Slocum, as if daring him to do more than wave around the lighted dynamite. Slocum knew in a flash he could never bluff this man. Dark eyes fixed on his, daring him to even more foolish acts.

"If that's what you want," Slocum said, taking the challenge. "I have to oblige." He reached into his pocket and pulled out two sticks he had taped together. Slocum tossed the explosive into the fire. The few braves daring to return from their previous headlong flight shrieked and ran for cover again.

Sherum continued to stare coldly at Slocum. With deliberate

movement, the Walapai walked to Monty Kelson and kicked the man in the ribs. To Slocum's surprise, the miner moaned weakly and his bloodshot eyes fluttered open. Moira's brother was tougher than he had any right to be.

"Here," Slocum said, tossing the lit bundle to the Walapai chief. This startled Sherum. He automatically reached out and grabbed the dynamite. Shocked at what he had done, he stared at it, not knowing what to do next with the deadly parcel.

Slocum had only an instant to act—and he did. Two quick strides brought him in front of the chief. He drew back his fist and let fly with a powerful haymaker. The blow caught Sherum in the belly and doubled him over.

"The dynamite," moaned Monty Kelson. "It's gonna blow!"

Slocum scooped up the bundle Sherum had dropped. The fuse burned down to only fractions of an inch from the detonating cap. Slocum tossed it underhanded into the night. The explosion snapped his teeth shut and momentarily stunned him. Slocum recovered fast and he worked to cut Kelson's bonds.

"Can you walk?"

"I kin run like the very devil hisself was after me," the miner assured him. "But my sister's—"

"Here I am, Monty!" Moira called. She rushed up. Slocum had to swing about and punch Sherum again. The Walapai chief had struggled to a sitting position and fumbled for the long knife sheathed at his belt. The red-haired woman's eyes went wide, as if she realized for the first time the seriousness of their predicament.

"We're not out of here, not by a dozen rows of apple trees," Slocum said, grabbing Kelson's arm and pulling the miner to his feet. As Slocum had feared, the miner's words were tougher than his body. Monty Kelson's strength dwindled and he sank to his knees, unable to support himself.

Ducking, Slocum got the man's arm around his neck. He lifted and helped Kelson away from the fire where the other sticks of dynamite sizzled and started to bubble.

"It'll explode!" Moira's hand went to her mouth in horror. "Do something. We're going to be blown to bits!" She had turned to stone, unable to do anything but stare at the two sticks of dynamite heating in the fire.

"Don't worry about it, not yet," Slocum said. "I used to put frozen dynamite in a skillet and fry it until it thawed."

"It *will* blow soon. Kin tell from the way the paper's all black and bubbly around the sticks," Monty Kelson said.

"What are we going to do?" asked Moira. Shock faded and she began edging away from the fire, going back in the direction where she had been held prisoner.

Slocum headed her off, herding her toward the Walapai horses. What had been out of the question a few minutes earlier now seemed possible. The braves had scattered when he walked in with the lit bundle of explosives. The braves standing guard over their remuda had vanished into the night along with the others. But that small advantage would evaporate quickly when Sherum regained consciousness or the Walapais overcame their fear of the dynamite.

"Get your brother slung across one of those horses," Slocum said. "It doesn't matter which one." Slocum wanted to force Moira into action and away from making decisions that might cost them their lives—such as to delay in choosing just the right mount. He waited until Moira struggled with Monty Kelson and decided there were better things to do than help her. If her brother flopped over the back of an Indian pony, fine. If not, he would get left to die.

It was a cruel decision, but it was the only way Slocum saw of getting free. He valued his scalp—and he did not want Moira Kelson falling into Walapai hands now.

He had shamed Sherum in front of his braves, as well as

forcing the rest of the war party to run into the night like frightened squaws. Either of those reasons would have been ample for the Walapai to torture Moira for long days, weeks, even months. She would beg for a death that would be denied her unless Slocum got her away from the camp.

Two warriors popped up in front of him, as if they grew from the ground like nocturnal mushrooms. Slocum kicked out and caught one in the kneecap, eliciting a yowl of pain. He drew his Colt Navy and fired point-blank into the other's body. Looking past the downed pair, Slocum tried to get a good shot at Chief Sherum. If he could drop the Walapai leader, this might create enough confusion to let him escape.

Sherum was nowhere to be seen, but in the distance Slocum heard a strong, commanding voice rallying the war party. He spun and raced back to the horses. Moira had mounted and her brother sat astride another horse.

"I told you to get him belly down like a sack of flour over the back of one of those nags," Slocum said irritably. No matter what he said, Moira Kelson ignored it and did what she wanted. This would get them all killed.

"I kin ride, mister."

"The name's John Slocum. You might as well know it before we all die."

"I won't fall off. I kin ride with the best," Monty Kelson insisted. Even as the words left his lips, he almost fell over. He grabbed at the horse's reins and clung for dear life. Kelson's moans of agony drowned out even the frightened neighing of the spooked horses.

"Ride," Slocum ordered. As he wheeled his mount about, an arrow sang through the night. He heard it whistle past his head and then lost sight of it in the dark. Bending low, he put his heels to the horse's flanks. The lack of saddle caused Slocum to slip as the horse twisted under him. He tried to regain his balance and failed.

Tumbling hard to the ground, Slocum lay for a moment, stunned. He blinked through a haze of pain and saw a dark outline rising above him. Reacting instinctively, he drew up his feet and kicked out like a mule. The impact of his boots against a muscular chest told him he had gained a brief instant's reprieve from death.

Slocum rolled to the side, then reversed direction quickly. A knife drove into the ground where he had been only an instant before. Scrambling to his feet, he faced a furious Walapai brave.

"Come here and die on my knife," the warrior invited.

Slocum had never drawn faster. His hand flew to his six-shooter. He cleared leather and got off the first shot before the Walapai took a step. The bullet caught the brave in the middle of the chest. But he didn't stop.

Lumbering forward and ignoring his wound, the brave slashed wildly with his knife. Slocum fired again, this time into the man's face. The Indian's head snapped back, and he finally had the good sense to die and stop threatening Slocum.

The entire fight had taken less than a minute but even a single heartbeat longer would have meant Slocum's death. Sherum had rallied his force and the Walapai were bearing down on Slocum from half a dozen different directions. He was ringed in by certain death.

Slocum fired twice more. Both shots missed. He started to squeeze the trigger again, but a brave stabbed at him from behind. Twisting about, Slocum used his six-gun as a club to smash into the Walapai's face. The Indian grunted in pain from a crushed nose and fell back.

Bracing his feet, Slocum prepared to meet the next warrior. The pounding of horses' hooves made him stand a little straighter. Moira Kelson rode hard in his direction, her head down next to her horse's and her heels raking constantly on the animal's heaving flanks. Her brash headlong charge scattered the Walapai again.

"Mr. Slocum, this way!" she shouted. Slocum didn't have to be told twice. Riding behind Moira was his only hope for escape.

He danced away from a knife thrust and barely avoided an arrow aimed at his legs. The Walapai wanted him alive so they could torture him. Slocum vowed that would never happen. He would force them to kill him cleanly in battle before he would surrender for lingering death.

"Ride like you mean it," Slocum shouted at Moira as he swung up behind her. "If we stay, we're goners."

She nodded, her coppery hair flowing back into Slocum's face with the movement. That long hair almost caused their deaths. Slocum instinctively brushed it from his eyes, carelessly sending it to one side. A brave sprinted up, grabbed a handful of hair and jerked hard, unseating Moira. Slocum's arms closed on her waist, and he dragged her back onto the horse.

"My hair! It hurts!" the woman screamed. She tried to loosen the warrior's hold on her hair but could not. The brave trotted alongside the horse, straining to jerk his victim from her seat.

Slocum used another round on the Indian, firing into the brawny forearm pulling Moira to the ground. Blood spurted, and the clutching hand twitched before opening enough to permit Moira her freedom. This threat passed, but another rushed down on them like an avalanche. Slocum fired into the approaching war party until his pistol came up empty. Then he concentrated on keeping his arm around the woman's slender waist and getting the hell away.

The horse tried to crow hop, but Slocum controlled it enough to start the all-out run into the darkness. Galloping full tilt at night was fraught with danger, but Slocum accepted the risk. The horse might step into an animal burrow and break a leg or stumble in a fall of rock. Those dangers paled in comparison with being caught by Sherum.

Slocum allowed the horse to gallop blindly for a few minutes. When the horse's flanks began heaving, lathering heavily, and the power in the strong pony's legs flagged, he reined back.

"Thanks for coming after me," Slocum said. "I hadn't expected it."

"It was the least I could do," Moira said. "You rescued Monty and me. I don't know how to thank you."

"You just did back there," Slocum said, urging the horse to a gait a little faster than a walk. Riding the pony into the ground had to be weighed against the Walapai overtaking them.

"Mr. Slocum, there's something else. We need you. Badly." She tried to turn, but Slocum kept his arms firmly around her, preventing much movement. Moira Kelson was quite an armful, and Slocum didn't want her falling off the horse. She had shown great horsemanship. She also had the distressing habit of turning to face him when she spoke. Not paying attention to the low-hanging branches brushing constantly against them would be painful—and dangerous.

No matter what, they had to keep riding as long as possible or Sherum's war party would capture them.

"We ride until we can't go on, then ride some more. With luck smiling on us, we can get out of here by dawn. Then we find the corporal and—"

"There's more, Mr. Slocum. Monty. My brother, he—" Moira swallowed hard. Slocum felt a tremor pass through her slender body and knew bad news was coming.

"What happened?"

"He was shot in the back by an arrow right after he got on the horse. Monty is sore in need of a doctor. Or someone skilled in removing such barbaric missiles from human flesh. Are you able to help him? If not, we must find a place where he can regain his strength until we can ride on.''

"The Walapai will find us if we do that," Slocum said. "We ride or die."

"Then leave us behind. Help us find a hiding place, then go after your corporal. We will be all right until you return with aid.'' Moira sat even straighter in the saddle, pressing warmly against Slocum. He felt the firm beating of her heart against his arm and the pressure of her buttocks against his groin moving in rhythm with the horse's gait. None of this ought to have affected his decision.

Moira Kelson was right. He ought to leave them behind. If he tried to do anything else, they would all die.

"I need to see how badly wounded your brother is. Where'd you leave him?"

"Along this trail, somewhere," Moira said, uncertainty in her voice.

Slocum didn't see any trail. Even if he had, how Monty Kelson could have followed it if he were injured as badly as Moira claimed would have required a miracle. Slocum hadn't noticed miracles happening too often this night. He reined back suddenly, stopping the horse. The thankful animal stood with its flanks heaving. Slocum strained to hear over its gusty breathing.

Behind, he heard the pounding of horses. The Walapai came after them. Only minutes separated Slocum from death by knife or arrow. Twisting around, he cocked his head to one side. Another sound filtered through the thick stand of pines upslope.

"That way," Slocum said, homing in on the distant noises. "That's got to be your brother."

"What if it isn't?" asked Moira. "I am confused, turned around. He might be over that way." She pointed down the mountainside. "I just don't know."

Slocum put his spurs to the horse and got the pony struggling uphill. He might be riding into the teeth of a trap, but he had to rely on his judgment. He doubted the Walapai had reached that far in their pursuit. If he was wrong, he and Moira were dead. If he guessed right, they might find only her dead brother.

"Monty!" she cried. Moira struggled in the circle of Slocum's arms and kicked free to jump to the ground. Slocum narrowed his eyes, trying to see what the woman already had. He finally made out the nervous horse tied to a low-hanging tree limb. Under the tree lay Monty Kelson, rolled onto his side.

Slocum shuddered. An arrow protruded from the center of the miner's back. Even if he pulled it out, there was no way in hell Kelson could survive. Bleeding, punctured lung, severed spine—any of those injuries would be fatal.

"Montgomery, please," sobbed Moira. "Talk to me."

"What do you want me to say, colleen o'mine?"

"Monty!" She sobbed, clutching her brother with fierce determination. Kelson groaned in pain, and Slocum knew he could never abandon him. Dismounting, Slocum knelt beside the miner.

"This hurt?"

"Like the very demons of Satan are nibblin' at me back," Kelson said, his voice so low Slocum hardly heard.

"That's a good sign. You're still fighting. All right," Slocum said, coming to a quick and possibly suicidal decision. "We find a place to hole up."

"Them Injuns will ne'er miss us," the miner said. "They track too good."

Slocum had firsthand knowledge of Sherum's skill. He had no reason to think the Walapai chief was any less adept a tracker than he was at hiding his own trail.

"There's an overhang. Get your brother into it. I'll pile branches over you to keep you from being seen."

"Will that work?" Moira sounded incredulous. Slocum didn't blame her. This was a harebrained idea and one likely to spell all their deaths. Still, he had to try. Moira Kelson would never willingly abandon her brother while breath flared his nostrils, and Slocum wasn't going to leave her behind for the Walapai to capture again.

"Here, let me help." Slocum dragged Monty Kelson uphill to the rocky outcropping. The miner scooted back farther, then sighed. For a moment, Slocum thought their troubles were over, that the miner had died. But the bright green eyes fixed on him from the darkness put this to the lie.

Slocum shoved Moira into the small cubbyhole, then fetched branches to cover the small opening. He heard the pair stirring within, but the sound was no louder than that of a fox with its kits. Then there was only silence.

He grabbed a bushy plant and tugged hard, finally yanking it from the ground. Using this as a broom, he did his best to erase their trail. Then he worked downhill to where the horses contentedly cropped at grass.

The horses did not protest as he tied more bushy growth to their hooves. They lifted their hooves and tried to shake off the unwanted burden, but they were too exhausted to do more than weakly protest. After Slocum had done what he could to eliminate all signs that the horses had come to this spot, he swung up onto horseback and grabbed the other's reins.

"Let's go for a ride," he said, hearing the approaching Walapai. Slocum put his heels to the horse's flanks and rode off slowly, doing his best to ride on rocky areas and keep away from soft earth.

It wasn't much and a man of Sherum's ability wouldn't be fooled long. Slocum hoped only that he led the pursuit away from Moira and her brother.

7

The captured horse refused to go any farther without incentive. Slocum leaned over and gave the animal's rump a sharp swat. It neighed loudly and took off running, its pounding hoofbeats echoing through the still night. Rather than remain where he was, Slocum turned his mount in the opposite direction and tried to get as much speed as possible from the exhausted animal.

It collapsed under him in less than a mile.

He hoped the distance was enough to lead Sherum astray— or at least past where Moira and her brother hid. Slocum had headed out, not sure what he would do to get away. The two stolen horses proved too broken down to give him the kind of escape he had envisioned. With two horses, he had hoped to ride one, then switch to the other, giving the first a chance to recuperate from the hard ride.

Neither horse had been in any condition to ride by the time he left Moira and Monty Kelson. Now he was afoot and trying to avoid capture by the Walapai.

Slocum ducked down behind a lightning-struck stump and reloaded his six-shooter. This took all the ammo he had.

"Six shots," he muttered. He had no chance to fight off Sherum now. The best he might do was to kill the renegades' chief. Or reduce the odds against him. Slocum had been in tight places before and had never given up. He wasn't going to now.

Crouching behind the stump, he waited as patiently as he could. The few tricks used to hide his trail would be simple for the Walapai to decipher. The best he could hope for was that their war party would split up, part going after one horse and the rest following the one he had ridden into the ground. Against a handful, he had a chance. Slim, but a chance.

Slocum tensed when he heard voices nearby. The Walapai had come up almost on top of him and he had not known it. He shook himself fully awake. The rescue had taken all his energy, and he had drifted into sleep at the worst possible time. Hand on the butt of his six-gun, he peered around the stump to see a pair of braves advancing slowly. They took several seconds to study the ground, then moved with the unerring skill of a trained hound dog.

They passed him within a minute. Slocum stared at their broad backs and had two easy shots. But he did not take them. If he fired now he would bring Sherum and the rest down on his neck. Moving fast, Slocum rose, drew his Colt, and buffaloed the nearest brave. The other Indian swung about, rifle rising at the disturbance.

Before the smallest sound of surprise or warning escaped the man's mouth, Slocum swarmed all over him. He swung his six-shooter again but missed knocking the brave out. The barrel glanced off the side of the head, stunning him but not putting him out of the fight.

Weak struggles greeted Slocum as he recovered his balance

and moved in to finish the job he had started.

He almost died on the knife point rising like a serpent from the Indian's hand. No power accompanied the thrust, but Slocum had to jerk around to avoid being gutted. Falling heavily on the Walapai brave, Slocum got one hand around the brawny wrist clutching the knife and another on the man's windpipe.

Gurgling noises came from blue lips as Slocum squeezed harder and harder. If he had not struck the glancing blow, he knew he would have been dead. The brave was fresh, strong, and eager to kill the thief who had stolen horses and disgraced the entire war party by walking into camp to save their captives.

Slocum finished him off in time to scoop up the fallen knife and face the first warrior. The Walapai groped for his rifle. A flick of the wrist sent the knife Slocum had grabbed cartwheeling through the air. Life flowed out along with blood as the knife sank into the exposed chest.

Panting harshly, Slocum regained his composure. He retrieved the knife and then stripped both guns and ammo from the braves. They wouldn't need their rifles any more—and he did. As he stood over their bodies, he considered dragging them out of sight. The fight had taken too much energy from him. He left them, only thin grama grass masking their corpses from casual sight. He had no reason to think that Sherum would not find their bodies quickly and center the search in this area.

"Fine," Slocum said under his breath. "Let them come for me." If the Walapai hunted him, they might miss Moira and her brother.

For the next seven hours, Slocum used every trick he had learned or even heard about to throw off pursuit. The opportunity to kill more of the war party never presented itself, but he counted this as lucky. He was dog-tired, and his vision blurred from the fatigue. Any fight he had gotten into would have ended quickly with his death.

An hour before dawn, Slocum returned to the overhang where he had left Moira and Monty. He approached cautiously, straining hard to hear any possible danger. When he swung around and peered through the branches he had used to cover their hiding place, he caught his breath.

Monty Kelson lay on the hard ground under the outcropping, breathing harshly. Of his sister there was no sign.

Slocum started to shake the miner awake, then stopped when he saw small footprints leading away. He used the broken limb of a fir tree to wipe away the trail as he followed it. Slocum's initial worry turned to cold anger. When he found the red-haired woman, she was busy plucking weeds from under a tree.

"If I'd been a Walapai, you'd be dead—or worse," he said. The sound of his voice caused her to jump.

"Oh, John, you startled me."

"I could have done more if I'd been a Walapai. They are still looking for us."

"I heard horses during the night," Moira said, returning to her harvesting. "I feared it might be the war party rather than your cavalry troopers."

"Why did you leave the shelter?" Slocum's anger faded and wariness returned. Sherum stalked the mountains hunting for them. Slocum felt exposed and vulnerable, though he carried two captured rifles and a pocketful of ammunition.

"Monty's wound requires *some* tending. Since boiling water is out of the question, I decided to apply a poultice."

"With those weeds?" Slocum scratched his head.

"Why, they look like those back in Ireland I used. There are so many plants of a strange nature in these hills."

"Come on," he said. "And leave those. If you think your brother needs tending, we can use other medicine."

Moira reluctantly dropped the weeds she had gathered but

followed quietly, as a puff of wind blew through the predawn forest. Slocum hiked uphill until he came to the edge of a small glade. Here he found jimson weed growing in the shadier areas. He quickly stripped off a few dried blossoms and knocked loose a dozen seeds.

"These won't cure your brother, but they will ease his pain a mite."

"What do they do?"

"Indians use them in their medicine ceremonies. They see visions after chewing them. I've heard tell a few make the bad pain more tolerable."

"Thank you, John," she said. "You've done so much for Monty and me. It took me a while after you were gone, but I came to realize you saved our lives."

"Things have moved fast," he allowed. "We're still alive and kicking. That's what's important." Slocum said nothing about her brother. Monty Kelson would like as not never see another sunset—or even a sunrise.

"You're so modest. John, you *saved* our lives." Moira moved closer. He felt the heat of her body as if the door of a stove had opened. She moved still closer. Her breasts pressed into his chest as she gazed up into his eyes.

Green eyes met green. Seldom had he seen a woman so lovely, so alluring, so wanting to be kissed. He bent over. Her eyes closed and her ruby lips parted slightly. They kissed. At first it was soft, easy, an exploration rather than passion. This changed quickly as Moira's arms circled Slocum's body and held him tight. He quickly found himself with a hot-blooded woman putting all her emotional needs into a kiss.

Desire flared and Slocum knew they had reached the point of no return. It was foolish to stand in the glade like this with dozens of murderous Walapai renegades hunting them, but Moira wasn't to be denied—and Slocum wasn't going to try.

Her tongue darted from between her lips and lightly brushed

his. Then it boldly intruded into his mouth where their tongues dueled erotically. Slocum felt the rise and fall of Moira's firm breasts increase as her desires mounted. His hands stroked over her back, drifted lower and cupped her buttocks.

He pulled her even closer. As he did, he felt the familiar tension in his own loins grow. It had been a spell since he had been with a woman, and even longer since he had been with one as lovely and beguiling as Moira Kelson.

He gasped when the woman's hand stroked over his chest and came to rest over the developing bulge at his crotch. She squeezed rhythmically and flashed him a wicked smile.

"Give you any ideas?"

"I've had ideas since the first time I saw you in Prescott," Slocum said.

"Now's the chance to put those ideas into practice, luv."

She tilted her head back as his kisses moved from her face to her silken white throat. He kissed and licked and moved lower, his tongue pushing apart the buttons on her blouse one by one. Gradually, he exposed her breasts. It took some fumbling but he pushed away the frilly undergarment hiding her luscious bosoms.

Like alabaster mountains they rose from her chest, capped with cherry-red nipples. Slocum sucked one hard cap into his mouth and rolled his tongue over it. Moira gasped and went weak in the knees. He followed her to the ground and then moved to the other nipple, giving it the same treatment.

"You excite me, John. I never felt like this before." Moira's hands tore at his shirt to get it off, then worked frantically to free his gun belt. Slocum had to help her with this, but his eyes were fixed on her naked breasts bobbing gently in the first light of dawn. Those snowy hills beckoned for him to climb them and claim them as his territory.

He groaned as she succeeded in opening the buttoned fly of

his jeans. His erection sprang forth, hard and freed of its cloth prison at last.

"So big, so very big," she said, her eyes wide as she stared at his groin. Then she looked into his eyes and said, "I want it in me, John. I need it so!"

He was not going to deny her something he wanted, also. But Slocum found she wasn't inclined to let him simply push up her skirts and sate their runaway passions. The woman wanted more. Her hands cupped his buttocks again and pulled him upward on her chest as she lay back in the soft grass.

"Yes, like that, John. Oh, you feel so good against my breasts."

He straddled her waist, his thick manhood resting between the mounds of flesh. Reaching down, he pushed on the outer slopes of her bosoms, crushing the soft flesh down around his length. He gasped in surprise when he felt a light, damp touch on the very tip of his organ. Moira craned her neck upward and let her pink tongue flick forth like a snake's. She teased the very end until he backed off.

"Forward. Come forward again and get some more," she said enticingly.

Slocum obeyed. He liked the way she surrounded him, her soft breasts throbbing with vitality. More than this he liked the feel of her tongue on the very end of his manhood. His hands stroked up and down the sleek slopes of her breasts until neither of them could stand an instant more of this tantalizing motion.

Slocum reached down and swept up her skirts, exposing long legs. Moira lifted them on either side of his body and parted them wantonly, inviting Slocum in. He moved quickly. For a moment he felt the sensitive end of his shaft brush the coppery thatch between her legs, then all rational thought was swept away as he stroked forward.

Totally surrounded by clutching female flesh, he found himself acting like a young buck with his first woman. Moira's legs locked around his waist, drawing him ever deeper into her moist interior. She thrashed about, moaning loudly. Somewhere in the back of his mind he worried the Walapai might hear them. Then even this vague misgiving on his part vanished like the night running from dawn.

Faster and faster he moved as Moira coaxed him to a rhythm that satisfied them both. When he could no longer stand the pressures mounting within, he gasped and spilled his seed. But he was seconds behind the woman in the release of mutual craving for one another.

Slocum supported himself on his arms and gazed into her face. He had thought Moira Kelson beautiful before. Now she showed the radiance of an angel come to earth.

"Consider this payment for rescuing us," she said.

Slocum shoved back and began to get dressed. He felt a pang of disappointment in her words, but had no reason to expect more from her. Then he brightened as she added, "A *first* payment."

Almost primly she buttoned her blouse and smoothed her skirts. She stood and stared at the jimson weed seeds he had given her.

"Will these really help Monty?"

The question brought Slocum back to reality. He wasn't taking his best girl out for a Sunday picnic. Montgomery Kelson lay near death and a score of Walapai braves sought their deaths. Sherum had broken with Levy-Levy and brought the wrath of the bluecoats down on his head. The Walapai chief wasn't going to take kindly to anyone reporting his whereabouts to the cavalry.

And Slocum had done more than that to Sherum. He had wounded the chief's pride.

"They'll help him forget he's in so much pain," Slocum said. "More than that, well . . ." He shrugged. The miner was past needing a doctor. More likely, an undertaker would provide the next services Kelson required, if they got back to town without losing their own scalps. Still, Slocum had thought the tough miner was a goner before and Kelson kept surprising him.

He might survive long enough for Slocum to find Framingham's patrol and get back to Beale Springs.

False dawn passed and the sun began poking up over a distant ridge to bring the light of day into the narrow valley where they hid. They returned to the rock outcropping as the sun popped up fully over the trees.

For a moment, Slocum thought the miner had died. Then he heard a cough and desperate gasping again.

"Here, Monty. Mr. Slocum found these for you. Chew them."

"Crazy weed?" muttered the miner. Then Slocum saw understanding and acceptance. Kelson chewed the seeds slowly, then closed his eyes and let the alkaloid work its mind-twisting magic on him. Slocum had no idea what Kelson saw or heard on the seed, but the miner forgot his pain.

As he muttered to himself, Slocum examined Kelson's wound. The arrow had missed severing his spine by inches. That didn't make the wound any less serious—or fatal. It simply meant Moira's brother would linger for a while before he finally died.

"I can't remove the arrow," Slocum said. He snapped it off and threw the fletched end aside. "If I try, it'll rip him up inside far worse and kill him outright."

"Then let him sleep now. He needs rest. And so do we. Is it safe to sleep?"

Slocum lied and told her it was. She moved closer and curled up beside him. In minutes, Moira slept, her head in his lap. For the woman, sleep came quickly. Not so for Slocum. He heard every sound outside as morning feeding time came and went. Rabbits running and coyotes chasing, birds singing and insects chirping all mixed together, but he remained alert for the sound of approaching Walapai.

"Moira asleep?" came the whispered question.

"Reckon so," Slocum said, looking down at the woman. Her face had lost the lines of strain apparent earlier. She might have been a small child, so peacefully did she sleep.

"I ain't gonna make it much longer. Thank you kindly for the crazy weed. Doesn't do much for the pain, but somehow it don't matter as much to me."

Slocum had nothing to say to this. He thought he heard movement outside. He clutched one of the stolen rifles and waited for a brave to show himself. A ground squirrel ran past their shelter without even glancing in their direction. Slocum forced himself to relax. Staying keyed up for too long tired him out faster and robbed him of needed sharpness.

"You got two of them rifles. Leave me one and you take Moira out of here."

"We can all make it."

"That's not you talkin', Slocum. That's my sister. Never saw a woman so determined in all my life—or so sure of herself, even when she's flat-out wrong." Kelson coughed and tried to get more comfortable on the rocky floor of their sanctuary. Slocum saw the miner did not succeed.

"You and her hit it off good. Glad to see that. Moira's not taken a fancy to many men in her day. Choosy, real choosy."

"The cavalry patrol is around somewhere. Sherum will hightail it when he realizes he can't find us."

Kelson rambled on, ignoring Slocum.

"You get her on back to Prescott and safety. Sell off the Three Card Monte to whoever's dumb enough to buy a worthless hole in the ground, then see Moira off to Boston. We got some cousins there, just arrived from Ireland. They'll look after her good." Monty Kelson's eyes burned intensely.

" 'Less you intend carin' for her. She could do worse. So could you."

"I'll get her back to Prescott safe and sound," Slocum said. He hoped this wasn't a hollow promise. Even if it turned out to be, it satisfied a dying man. A small smile danced on Kelson's lips before he closed his eyes.

Again Slocum thought the miner had died, but the ragged breathing put this to the lie. All day Slocum and Moira sat in the cave, dozing and coming awake with a start, while Monty Kelson slept heavily until nightfall.

"What are we going to do, John?" Moira asked. "I'm hungry and thirsty and Monty's getting weaker by the minute."

"We have to fetch help. The cavalry patrol is out there," he said, knowing Framingham had intended to return to Beale Springs. The lie gave her some hope.

"I can defend myself with this," Kelson said in a surprisingly hearty voice. He clutched a rifle and used it to lever himself into a sitting position. "It's sundown. You and Slocum ought to light out now. The quicker you go, the quicker you'll get back."

Moira chewed on her lower lip, glancing from her brother to Slocum and then back. She wiped at tears rolling down her cheeks as she nodded agreement with the plan.

"Let's go," Slocum said. An uneasy feeling made him anxious to leave their shelter. Perhaps they had been too lucky in how the Walapai had missed them. Perhaps it was Slocum's sixth sense telling him trouble was on the way. Whatever the source, he felt better when Moira kissed her brother farewell and crawled into the twilight. Slocum paused before he followed.

Monty Kelson pulled the rifle across his lap.

"Go on now. Don't disappoint me."

Slocum smiled and left. Not getting killed—not letting Moira die—would please both the miner and Slocum.

"Which way?" the red-haired woman asked, turning in circles and unable to choose a direction.

"Upslope," Slocum said. "We go up and over the mountain. Don't know where that might take us, but it's away from the Walapai."

Slocum hefted the second rifle and patted the pocket filled with ammo, then started walking. Moira followed more hesitantly, looking back toward the shelter and her brother often until the Ponderosa pines swallowed them.

"He'll be all right, won't he, John?"

Before Slocum could answer, war whoops echoed up the hill. A shot rang out. Then a second and finally a ragged volley.

Long silence became Moira Kelson's answer.

8

"Monty!" Moira Kelson whirled and started back down the mountainside. Slocum grabbed her arm and fought for a moment to restrain her. She finally stopped trying to return and simply stared in the direction of the commotion.

"He's dead," Slocum said brutally. "This time he went out fighting. That's all he could have hoped for."

"We might have found a doctor. He was a strong man."

"You've got to be strong, too," Slocum said. "You have to go on, even knowing the Walapai killed him."

Slocum hoped the miner had taken more than a few of the Indians with him. It was little enough payment for the injuries inflicted on him while a prisoner. And no amount of killing short of complete extermination would repay them for the arrow in the back. Slocum had seen fatal wounds before, and this one would have killed Montgomery Kelson eventually, no matter how determined he had been.

"What are we going to do?" she asked.

Slocum didn't understand her question. "We stay alive," he said. "If we reach the ridge, we can get away. Standing here waiting for the Walapai to come after us will only get our scalps lifted."

"You're right." Moira heaved a sigh that lifted and dropped her breasts. Slocum had seen those sumptuous breasts, felt them, enjoyed them, and had received her promise there would be other times. He hoped Moira would be able to keep that promise.

They covered a mile toward the ridge before Slocum got the eerie feeling of being watched. Slocum reached out and took Moira's shoulder. He held his finger to his lips cautioning her to silence. He motioned for her to keep going along the same dirt track they had been following while he doubled back.

Slocum cut away from their path and found a large pine tree. He rested the rifle against the trunk and waited. In less than a minute, two shadows fluttered along the trail. Slocum's finger drew back, then relaxed when he realized the two braves were accompanied by at least one more. If he killed one, he would have the other two swarming all over him.

And Slocum would count himself as lucky if there were only two. The entire Walapai war party might be tracking them, after they had killed Monty Kelson.

Waiting another minute for more braves, Slocum satisfied himself these three were the only ones on their trail. His mind raced as he considered what to do. Almost before his brain came to a decision, his feet were moving. He drifted from one tree to the next, trailing the warriors so intent on Moira Kelson.

The trailing brave's attention was focused forward. He never suspected Slocum might be behind him. And that spelled his death. Slocum moved like lightning. Four quick steps closed the distance between him and the brave. The Walapai heard Slocum's boots crushing pine needles and swung about in time to catch the rifle butt in the chin. The man went down, stunned.

He never had a chance to do more than flail weakly. Slocum grabbed the brave's own knife and used it on an exposed throat. Bright blood flowed for a moment, then the Walapai's heart stopped pumping. He twitched feebly, like a dead snake waiting for sundown, then lay silent.

Slocum panted harshly and stilled his own emotions. It was never easy killing a man, even in self-defense. With Moira's life riding on his ability, Slocum felt added tautness in his gut. More than his own life depended on his skill now. If he failed, the fiery redhead joined her brother in death.

A scream cut through the stillness of the forested area. Slocum forced himself to maintain a steady, cautious approach. To bull in now spelled disaster.

"Let me go, you savage!" came Moira's shrill voice. A curt laugh was followed by a meaty *thunk*!

Then the woman screamed again. The shriek was cut off as suddenly as it had come. Slocum circled, homing in on the area where the Walapai had caught her. Even being careful, he almost overran the trio. One brave pinned Moira to the ground, his knees on her shoulders. She fought futilely against his weight and the hand over her mouth. The other warrior stood to one side, grinning at the woman's helplessness.

Again Slocum considered using the rifle to put a bullet in one attacker's head. And again he knew even a single shot might draw the rest of the war party down on them. Silence was his ally—and he wanted two more allies in silent, dead Indians.

The Walapai holding down Moira spotted Slocum first and shouted a warning to his friend. The standing brave whipped around, a war lance tracing a blurred arc as it swung in Slocum's direction. The silvered blade strapped at the end of the lance opened a shallow gash on Slocum's belly. Only instinct saved him from being gutted.

The warrior let out a war whoop and lunged forward with the lance. This time Slocum moved easily to one side, letting the deadly point slide past harmlessly. Slocum used the rifle barrel like a bludgeon. He clubbed the brave to his knees and kept hitting him until he lay on the ground, unconscious.

"John!" cried Moira. She struggled under the weight of the other brave, who had pulled his hand away from her mouth to better draw a six-gun shoved into his woven fabric belt.

Slocum dug his toes into the hard dirt and launched himself through the air. He crashed into the brave pinning Moira and knocked him to one side. Slocum was aware of Moira scrambling to her feet, but he had his hands full with a tussling Walapai fighter.

The Indian twisted and turned and gave Slocum a time until he got his hand around the brave's wrist. Twisting viciously, Slocum forced the six-shooter from his grip. Then they were rolling over and over. Slocum's fate suddenly came apparent. He banged his head against a half-buried rock. Like the brave he had buffaloed seconds earlier, he was now more insensate than aware. With the Walapai rising above him, he knew he was a goner.

Slocum saw the anticipation of an easy kill on the Walapai's face. A huge grin and a gleaming knife summed up Slocum's end.

Then the Walapai vanished. He was there one instant and gone the next. Slocum lay on his back staring through the pines at the blue Arizona sky and wondering if he had died and gone to heaven. Never had he thought heaven would be his destination after death, and he had never considered it might look like the place where he died.

Angels' voices came to him from a distance, calling his name and touching him lightly.

"John," they sang. "John!"

The sharper call caused him to stir. Immediate pain shot through his head and told him he had not died. Pushing to his elbows, he saw the Walapai laying across his legs, pinning him to the ground.

"What do I do now?" asked Moira Kelson. She held the rifle by its barrel. She had taken a swing at the warrior and walloped him on the back of the head with the stock. From the way the wood hung at a crazy angle from the receiver, Slocum guessed she had destroyed its usefulness as a weapon. But he wasn't complaining. She had saved his life.

The Indian she had slugged began to stir as Slocum regained his own senses. Slocum's hand gripped the knife at his belt, and he used it in a quick, death-dealing slash. But he was not finished with his slaughter. He returned to the Indian who had wielded the lance and dispatched him, too. Neither of his foes could be left alive, either to plague their footsteps or return to Sherum for reinforcements.

"Oh, John," Moira said, turning her head as he finished his gory work. Then she straightened her shoulders and looked back, cold determination etched on her gentle face. "You should have let me do that. He might have been the one who killed my brother."

"Don't know about that," Slocum said, "but they surely would have killed us. Thanks for pulling my bacon out of the fire."

She smiled weakly, then dropped the rifle and came to him. Her arms closed around him, and she began crying. Hot tears turned his shirt damp, but the quaking in her body subsided soon and she pushed back from him.

"I'm better now," she said. "This is all so . . . different for me."

"You live in Boston? Your brother asked me to see that you got back there."

Moira shrugged. "I don't live much of anywhere now. No real family, now that Monty is gone. We had two brothers and three sisters, but they all died." She began smoothing her dirty, wrinkled clothing. The grooming did little to change her appearance. In spite of the grime and tears, Slocum knew he had never seen a lovelier woman.

"They died, too," Moira went on, struggling to keep back the tears. "Cholera. Our parents had died years earlier in another epidemic. No one ever put a name to it."

"What will you do when we get back to Prescott?" Slocum asked, wanting to keep her mind away from the bodies around them and on the safety promised by civilization.

"Monty was talking about cousins in Boston. Fresh over from Ireland, they are, but I don't know them. When I was a wee baby they might have seen me, but I have no recollection of them. I am on my own, John."

"And?" Something about the way Moira said it puzzled him. There was no fear with this realization, but there was sorrow and something else he could not pin down.

"I am rather looking forward to it. Somehow, coming here to be with Monty shackled me. I was his responsibility. Now only I determine my future. If I want to go to San Francisco, I can. Or if I want to remain in Prescott, that, too, is within my power."

"Or if you want to return to Boston and your family, you can," Slocum finished.

"That is also possible," Moira said, staring at him with her emerald eyes. "There might be reasons, good ones, for staying in Arizona."

He looked away uncomfortably. He did not want to be the only reason she remained in Arizona Territory. There had to be more than corraling him. Slocum had long enjoyed the feeling of freedom Moira only dimly saw in her future. Traveling where the wind blew him, staying or moving on, the sky above his roof and the horizon a destination, this was his way of life and not one he wanted to share with a woman.

Even one as lovely as Kelson.

"From the way the land rises up in front of us," Slocum said, "the ridge isn't too far off. The quicker we get there, the quicker we can be down the far side of the mountain and on our way to Prescott."

"How far is it?"

Slocum shook his head. Meandering around the twisting, turning byways of the canyons turned a five-day ride from Prescott into a week or longer. From Beale Springs the Three Card Monte Mine had been a grueling three-day ride for the cavalry, but he thought it might be quicker on foot for them to get to Prescott.

"A lot of dusty, waterless miles," Slocum said. "We've got a mountain to crawl over that no horse could climb. That cuts a passel of miles off our travel but slows us down."

"Will they come for us?" Moira glanced over her shoulder at the two dead Walapai stretched on the ground. Slocum knew she meant the others in the war party.

"They might. If Sherum rode out of camp the same time these came for us, he might be around the mountain about the same time we get down the far side."

Moira shuddered at the prospect of encountering Sherum again. Slocum picked up the pace, although the mountain began rising up more steeply with every step they took. By midday they were scaling sheer rock faces and that night they camped precariously on a small ledge overlooking the valley.

Moira said nothing, but Slocum knew she tried to spot where her brother had died and his mine from their aerie. His attention focused more on their back trail and whether the Walapai war party tracked them.

Slocum suspected both he and Moira failed to satisfy themselves.

• • •

"I'm mighty hungry, John. And thirsty, too. The drink from the spring didn't go very far in quenching my thirst." Moira rubbed her belly to emphasize her need.

"Best to keep moving. We can find another spring before long. These mountains have plenty of water running through them." The sun tipped past midday and headed for the towering canyon wall. Light would fade in a few hours, bringing night far too soon for Slocum's comfort. They had scaled the peak and gotten down into the canyon leading out of the mountains but were not safe yet.

Sherum roamed these rocky byways and might turn up at any time. It might take days for him to circle the mountain they had climbed in a day's time, but the war chief rode stolen horses and he and Moira were footsore and exhausted.

"When we find the road to Prescott, then we can rest a mite," he promised.

"I'm getting dizzy from lack of food, John," she complained. "And water. My mouth is filled with cotton wool."

"Here," Slocum said, spotting some wild blackberries growing on a thorny shrub. "Eat some of these. They'll give you some moisture and something to chew on while we walk."

"I'm tired," she complained. "Can't we rest, just for a few minutes?"

Slocum grew restive. He needed a respite and he needed water, but he felt Sherum breathing down his neck. The quicker they got to Prescott, the sooner they could relax.

"For a few," Slocum agreed. He picked more berries and divided them with Moira. The redhead eagerly devoured the berries, getting blue juice on her dress. The stains were hardly noticeable amid the dirt and dried blood already there.

After finishing his sparse meal, Slocum got to his feet and prowled about, eyes returning to the peak they had scaled. It hardly seemed possible they had made such good time getting over that mound of rocks. Necessity had driven them, but self-preservation would drive Chief Sherum. Slocum wondered if Sherum had abandoned his camp and moved on or if the Walapai hunted them down. He wondered if he would ever simply rest again without constant vigilance.

"John? John!" The sharpness in Moira's voice brought Slocum running. She pointed through the trees at six braves riding slowly as they studied the ground.

"Get down," he said, pulling the woman behind a tree. He felt her heart pounding as she pressed close to his side. "They'll ride past, and we'll be all right," he said. But Slocum was fingering his Colt and wondering if the six rounds remaining there would be enough.

They had to be.

"They're not going away. They've stopped. They found something!"

"Don't panic. It'll only mean trouble," Slocum said, but sweat beaded on his forehead. The day was warm, but his reaction came from the way the Walapai refused to ride on. What had they seen? Slocum and Moira had not walked over that patch of ground, so the war party couldn't have found their track. But they had obviously found something of interest from the way three of them huddled around, hunkered down and ran fingers back and forth on the ground.

One brave still on horseback hissed and drew the others' attention. The three jumped onto their horses but did not ride off.

"What's going on, John? They haven't seen us, so what are they doing?"

Slocum had no answer. If he ventured from the hiding place, he might draw their notice, yet curiosity was getting the better of him. He silently motioned for Moira to stay low, then moved quietly toward the braves.

The closer he got to the Walapai, the more his curiosity burned. They sat silently, eyes fixed at some point down the valley. Slocum rose and tried to see what held them frozen like statues outside a courthouse.

Something betrayed Slocum and caused the nearest brave to let out a cry and trigger a round from his rifle. The slug tore past Slocum's head and sent him diving for cover. He fumbled to draw his six-shooter, knowing every shot had to count.

Aiming his six-gun, Slocum swung around to get the best shot he could. The sharp report made him jump. He stared at his Colt Navy in surprise. He hadn't fired, and neither had the Walapai.

"Charge!"

Along with the loud command came the tooting of a cavalry bugle. The thunder of hooves followed closely after. Slocum craned his neck and saw the approaching dust cloud. He took three quick shots, not worrying about hitting any of the war party but more concerned with slowing their escape.

Two of the braves began firing rapidly in his direction. Leaves and splinters from branches flew all around him. Slocum went back to ground, burying his face in the dirt. He winced as hot lead ran past his shoulder, but the other slugs passed him by.

"After them, take them!" came the cry from the cavalry's commander. Slocum recognized Captain Thomas Byrne's voice.

More slugs tore through the foliage around Slocum. He got off his last three shots. The hammer fell on an empty chamber, but the Walapai were not hightailing it. They turned their fire toward him rather than fleeing the soldiers. A new lance of pain slashed through Slocum's leg.

"Aieee!" The Walapai warriors made their decision. They

rode down on Slocum. He was unable to stand because of the leg wound.

Slocum watched death approaching. He couldn't run, and Byrne's troopers were still too far away to do any good.

9

"Stop, you don't want him. You want *me*!"

"Moira, get down!" shouted Slocum. But the woman did not pay any heed to his warning. She shouted and waved her arms to draw attention away from Slocum. Perhaps she thought he needed time to reload—he had no more bullets. Or she might have believed he could save them both if she distracted the Walapai.

Whatever her reason, it worked. The war party turned their rifles in her direction, giving Slocum a chance to return Moira's favor. In the few seconds the braves were diverted from their original target, Slocum got his leg under him and lumbered forward. He couldn't reach the nearest rider, but he threw himself headlong into the Indian's mount. The horse reared in reaction to the impact, pawing frantically at Slocum with its front hooves.

This threw the rider to the ground and confusion spread

among the remaining warriors. Their horses reared and forced them to stop firing.

"Get them, men. No quarter!" came Byrne's command echoing through the woods from down the valley. A ragged volley further frightened the Walapais' horses. Slocum leaped onto the brave on the ground and wrestled with him, but the Indian proved too agile an opponent and fought free. A quick look convinced the brave of the hopelessness of fighting. He lit out through the woods, dodging and twisting to avoid the cavalry's increasingly accurate fire as the troopers neared.

The other Walapai in the war party scattered; Byrne ordered two squads after them.

"One's making his way through the woods," Slocum got out as the captain rode over. He tried to point but his arm refused to lift. He had been through too much in the past days and now his strength abandoned him completely. He sank to the ground and stared up at the cavalry officer.

"That's all right, Slocum. We'll track them down. Have you seen Chief Sherum?" Byrne was all business, no hint of alcohol fogging his faculties. For that Slocum was glad. A drunken officer meant more problems when it came to chasing down the renegades.

Slocum nodded and nodded in Moira Kelson's direction. "Her brother died with a Walapai arrow in his back." Slocum hesitated to say any more about how Sherum had tortured Monty Kelson. His sister had been through hell. Reminding her of it now was cruel.

"He's not the only one to have died," Byrne said. "The other miner died, also. Word came from Dr. Gavilan before we left Beale Springs."

Moira sobbed softly. Slocum had no idea if she had known her brother's partner well or if this was simply the last link in her life snapping away.

"Who owns their mine?" Slocum asked.

The captain shook his head. "I cannot say. That's a civil matter. I am entrusted with stopping Sherum as quickly as possible. Orders have come down from the Bureau of Indian Affairs *and* the War Department. Both agree."

Slocum snorted. This might be the first time those two battling organizations had ever agreed on any Indian policy. Chief Sherum had tweaked the noses of the powerful back in Washington by refusing to abide by terms of the treaty signed by Levy-Levy. Making the politicians look bad was worse, in their minds, than the rampage that had resulted in so many deaths.

Looking at Moira, Slocum knew no amount of justice could be brought to Sherum that would return her brother's life or that of his partner.

"Captain," called a returning trooper. "We run three of the bastards to ground. The others got clean away."

Slocum watched the anger cloud Byrne's face. Then the officer pushed it away. "Very good. Are the three captured or dead?"

"Dead, sir."

"No hope of finding the others?"

"Sir, they slipped away without a trace. It would take another Injun to track them."

"Is that so, Slocum?" asked Byrne. "Are you up to the chore?"

"I need to get some gear, Captain, and get my injuries patched up. After we see Miss Kelson back to the camp, then I'll head on out again." Slocum watched as Byrne thought on the matter. The captain nodded, lifted his arm and motioned for the cavalry to form a column behind the gently fluttering blue and gold banner.

"Are we to walk back, John?" asked Moira. "We can't keep up if they ride off, now can we?"

"I'll see to it." Slocum caught up with Byrne and spent a

few minutes discussing the matter. The best the captain would do was allow Slocum and Moira to ride a captured Walapai pony back to Beale Springs. Although they rode in silence, lost in their own thoughts, Slocum didn't mind too much. He got to ride with his arms around the lovely woman again, and now and then, she leaned back tiredly against him. The pressure of her body against his reminded him of the time they had spent together—and how she had declared it was only the beginning for them.

"Never thought I'd see your ugly face again, Slocum," said Lieutenant Gorman. The man leaned against a hitching post, picking his teeth with the tip of a large knife. "Had a bet that Sherum would eat you alive." At his feet growled the abused yellow dog.

"It'd give him a bellyache," Slocum said, jumping down. Moira frowned at the exchange. He helped her down and guided her away from the obnoxious lieutenant.

"Why was he so rude to you, John? I thought you worked as scout for the post."

"I do. Some folks don't cotton much to me. Might have something to do with the people I associate with." Slocum nodded in Walapai Charley's direction. The Indian scout smiled slightly, then tugged down the broad felt brim of his floppy hat and leaned back, feigning sleep. Slocum knew the scout watched Moira's every move.

For all that, there were few men at Beale Springs not watching as they entered the captain's office.

Moira sat in the only chair other than Byrne's, hands in her lap primly. The dirt on her face and the tears in her clothing did nothing to diminish her beauty.

"How long are we to be here, John? I would like to bathe and find more clothing. The rest of my belongings were at the mine. I fear they are all gone."

Slocum tried to remember seeing anything at the Three Card Monte Mine that might have belonged to Moira and couldn't. She had lost all her possessions in the Walapai raid.

"That will be taken care of, Miss Kelson," said Byrne, striding into his office. He dropped his cap on the desk and sat heavily. For a moment, Slocum thought the officer was going to open a drawer and pull out a bottle. He had a thirsty look in his eye, but Byrne did not succumb.

"Will the post sutler help her get what she needs?"

"She can talk with some of the officers' wives and see what they might find for her." Byrne paused, obviously considering this a dismissal Moira ought to honor immediately.

"Go on," Slocum said. "I'll see how you're getting along later." He saw that Byrne wanted a few words with him, and Slocum thought he knew what they might be from their brief exchange out in the mountains.

"Ma'am," Byrne said, rising as the red-haired woman left. She hesitated at the door, gave Slocum a wan smile, and then vanished into the heat outside.

"Now, Slocum, we need to find Sherum quickly. His violation of the treaty is raising hob all around the territory," Byrne said. "Sherum has taken it into his head to kill miners and raid stagecoaches. We fear he is growing bolder and might attack a town."

"He's certainly murdering miners," muttered Slocum.

"We need to track him down and stop him right away," Byrne said, not hearing Slocum's aside. "We are feeding Chief Levy-Levy's tribe from our post, and they have no need to hunt. We must convince Sherum he can also partake of the government's largesse."

"The camp here is providing food?" Slocum held back his contempt for this policy. He had seen it fail repeatedly, and the government never knew why. Who at Beale Springs was stealing the Walapai food and selling it on the black market?

"We are. Ah, come in, come in." Byrne motioned to Lieutenant Gorman and Walapai Charley. The officer crowded in first and snapped to attention in front of his commanding officer. The Indian scout leaned indolently against the wall, near Slocum.

"You still beating his dog for him?" Slocum asked Charley. The scout shook his head slightly and crossed his arms, the picture of complete indifference to what went on in the office.

"At ease, Lieutenant," Byrne said. Again, Slocum saw the captain's eyes drift toward a lower desk drawer, as if thirst were overpowering him. And again, Byrne did not reach for the bottle that must be there. "You know the situation with the Walapai. I want you, Gorman, to provide support for Slocum and Charley."

"Sir, I—" Samuel Gorman frowned and worked hard to think of new protests. "That would not be appropriate."

"I think having Sherum's half brother find him is very appropriate. Justice, as it were," Byrne said.

"You mean Charley's related to Sherum?" This startled Slocum.

"Every family's got a black sheep in it," Walapai Charley said, grinning crookedly. "Reckon I'm it in ours."

Slocum had to laugh. Neither Gorman nor Byrne cracked a smile at this small joke.

"Form a detachment, Lieutenant, and see that they are given the chance to track down our renegades. There will be no more killing and looting by Sherum and his band," Byrne said firmly. "Bring them back to Beale Springs so we can properly care for them—or bury them where they fall. Let the choice be theirs."

"Sir," said Gorman, saluting. He did an about-face and marched out. He did not look at either Slocum or Walapai Charley.

Slocum wondered at the lieutenant's reaction to being sent on patrol. Garrison duty was dull and most officers saw their chance for glory and advancement in the field. Capturing or killing Chief Sherum would be a feather in any officer's cap.

"I want them stopped," Byrne said. "Now get on out of here and do your jobs." He was reaching for the bottom drawer of his desk before Charley and Slocum left. They stood outside the captain's office and looked around the small post. Beale Springs sported only a waist-high fence circling it, more to keep the livestock in than attacking renegades out. Fort Whipple had a more extensive defensive perimeter, and the adobe buildings there were larger.

"That's the food line," Walapai Charley said. He lifted his chin to indicate a crowd of Walapai shoving to get closer to the post sutler's warehouse. "They pass out food this time every day."

"They ought to let them all starve," came an angry voice. Slocum turned to see a private clutching a shovel. The man's knuckles were white with tension as he gripped the handle. "Let every last one of them sons o' bitches die."

"Take away hunting land, what's left for the Walapai?" asked Charley. "You try starving them, and they'll join Sherum. Chief Levy-Levy won't have any control at all over them."

"Bullets are cheaper than giving them food," the private said.

"McCue!" came Lieutenant Gorman's sharp command. "Get mounted. We are riding with these two scouts."

Private McCue glowered, but Slocum couldn't tell where the young man's wrath was directed. Definitely at the Walapai waiting for their daily rations, but probably at Walapai Charley and perhaps even at Slocum. Morale at Beale Springs had changed in the weeks Slocum had been gone.

"Did the mood change when the Walapai started getting the food?" Slocum asked.

Charley shrugged. "Always bad blood. Maybe it got worse then. That one. John McCue. He is an angry young man. He has no good words for any Indian. But that is all right."

"Why?" asked Slocum.

Walapai Charley looked solemn and said, "We do not like him, either." Then he laughed and slapped Slocum on the shoulder. "Come, you need a fresh mount. That broke-down old nag you rode in on must have been my brother's. Sherum never could steal good horses."

They walked to the corral. Slocum slowed as he saw McCue and Gorman at the rear of the sutler's warehouse. They argued with the sutler, a burly man with a beard thicker than grizzly fur. The sutler started to grab McCue, but McCue pushed him away and reached for his six-gun. This forced the sutler to back off but did nothing to quell his anger.

Everyone appeared to hate everyone else at Beale Springs.

"There, take your pick. You might look to that horse," suggested Charley. "It is sturdy and needs little water."

"Any reason I shouldn't pick the paint?" Slocum eyed the horse Charley indicated, but the paint had stronger legs and a broad chest. Given the chance, that horse might run for miles before getting winded.

"Go on," Charley said, and Slocum wondered at the sly look that flashed across the scout's face. It was gone in an instant, and Slocum might have read something that wasn't there. He doubted it, though.

Leading the paint from the corral, he found a spare saddle and convinced the camp armorer to give him a rifle and ammunition. Charley nodded in agreement with asking for spare ammo.

"We hunt. No food from Beale Springs," he declared.

"Why not?"

"None to spare. What is not taken by the soldiers is given to the Walapai."

Slocum swung into the saddle and settled his gear. The paint stepped lively under him. Slocum thought he would enjoy this scout. The horse was strong and the search for Sherum challenging.

"That's my—" Private McCue's protest was cut short by a backhand blow from Lieutenant Gorman. McCue dropped to one knee and started to stand. Gorman moved closer. At the snap of Gorman's fingers, his big yellow dog came up and snarled at the private until the downed man acknowledged defeat.

"That's one fierce dog," Slocum said.

"You and Charley get out on the trail. Work your way north, toward the Colorado. Check watering holes. We want to stop Sherum before he kills any more innocent people." Gorman kicked at his dog, forcing it away.

"White eyes," Charley muttered under his breath so only Slocum could hear. "He wants to stop us from killing more white-eye miners."

"You know the springs about ten miles north and west from here?" said Gorman.

"No, but I reckon we can find the place," Slocum allowed.

"Start there. Look for any sign Sherum has ridden by recently. He is taunting us. We'll catch up with you before sundown."

"All right, Lieutenant." Slocum tugged on the reins and got the paint moving. Walapai Charley followed a few yards back, riding an old mare that had seen better days.

After they had ridden out of sight of Beale Springs, Charley said, "Byrne has much trouble in his ranks. Drinking will do nothing to cure the problems."

"Saw how thirsty he was," Slocum said, "but when he came riding up to rescue Miss Kelson and me, he was everything I could have wanted in a cavalry officer.''

"A good man. In your war he fought bravely and was given this post as reward. He has not shown any skill except for drinking after reaching Fort Whipple.''

"If he captures Sherum, it will mean a promotion,'' Slocum said. "I heard it in Byrne's voice. He wants this one bad.''

All afternoon they rode, Slocum's mind more on the post at Beale Springs and Moira Kelson than tracking. Walapai Charley occasionally dismounted, but Slocum couldn't tell if the scout hunted for spoor or went into the bushes to take a leak. It hardly mattered since Slocum doubted Sherum would come this close to the post. After the renegades scored a few more victories and became emboldened, perhaps, but not yet. Not after Byrne had killed or chased off six warriors and prevented Moira's recapture.

"Why'd the lieutenant send us here?'' Slocum wondered aloud as they rode toward the watering hole. Springs popped out of the ground all over the place. Some spewed sulfur and more than a few were hot springs, none good for drinking.

"Gorman might have wanted us out of his hair,'' Walapai Charley said. "He dislikes you and hates me.''

"Or there might be signs of the war party here,'' Slocum said, swinging off the paint. He walked about, studying the muddy ground. Most of the terrain was chopped up from horses' hooves—shod horses. No Indian pony had left these tracks.

As Slocum was about to comment on this, he saw the glint of metal. The setting sun was in his eyes, but he could never mistake the blued steel of a rifle barrel.

"Charley, get down!'' he shouted.

Slocum's warning came a fraction of a second too late. A bullet tore through the still twilight and knocked Walapai Charley from the saddle. And then the same hidden sniper turned his attention to Slocum. Bullets sang, and Slocum was forced to dive behind a fallen log out in the open a dozen paces from the nearest bubbling hot springs.

Pinned down as he was, he had little chance against his unseen attacker.

10

Slocum tried to figure out what he was going to do. If he stayed in one spot too long, the sniper would fill him full of holes. A simple move a few yards one way or the other might put Slocum squarely in the rifle sights—he didn't know where to dodge until he figured out where the marksman hid.

A tongue of orange flame jumped from the middle of a creosote bush, and Slocum had the sniper located. He fingered his Colt Navy and knew shooting into the brush would do little good. A better shot awaited him, one that might eliminate the problem permanently. All he had to do was find it. As he got his feet under him to make a dash for a low wash running past the bubbling springs, he froze.

A dog barked ferociously.

Almost as soon as it began, the barking stopped. But the sound warned Slocum he might face two attackers, not one. His eyes darted from side to side, from the bush where one rifleman lay in wait and then in the direction of the noisy dog.

"Now, Slocum, run for it now!" came the unexpected call from his left. Slocum saw Walapai Charley pulling himself upright and using a cottonwood to shield himself from the sniper.

"There're two of them," Slocum warned. He swung about, drew and fired twice into the creosote bush, knowing even this brief exchange would cause all hell to break loose. The ambushers now knew they had failed to kill Charley. That meant they had to rush their attack or risk getting plugged in a protracted gunfight.

Sure as rain, Slocum's quick flurry of slugs into the bush produced a new reply—from the direction of the barking dog. Walapai Charley fired his six-shooter at the second sniper and let Slocum roll to the side and come up behind a tree ten feet away, giving a better shot at the man in the bushes. Slocum snapped off two more rounds, then hesitated to fire blindly any more. He had two shots left before he had to reload. He wanted them to count.

The sound of movement alerted him to the sniper's retreat. Slocum rushed forward, throwing caution to the winds. He kicked through the creosote bush's low limbs and found a slight depression in the soft dirt where the gunman had lain in wait. The twilight made tracking slower, but Slocum guessed the sniper's direction of retreat.

He plunged ahead, thinking the sniper would not be cagey enough to lay a second trap. Slocum arrived at a deep, narrow arroyo in time to see the hunched-over rider whipping his horse to get away. Slocum used his two remaining rounds and missed with both.

Reloading, he quickly returned to find Charley gingerly rubbing his leg. This gunfight was over, too, with the same result.

"Danged bushwhacker almost got me. Busted a perfectly good knife." A bullet had hit smack in the middle of his sheath, then deflected off the knife blade.

Slocum nodded, then silently returned to study where the sniper had waited for him. Nearby, he found a small bit of blue fabric caught on a prickly-pear cactus thorn. Examining it in the fading light convinced him it was from a cavalry uniform.

He rejoined the Indian scout. Charley was at the far side of the clearing, pointing at tracks.

"Paw prints. A big dog, 'bout the size of Ulysses," Charley said.

"Sam Gorman's dog, the one he paid you to beat," Slocum said. "Reckon the lieutenant's scheme backfired. If his dog hadn't barked, we'd have never known there were two snipers."

"Why would the lieutenant want us dead?" Charley scratched his head. "He don't cotton much to me, but he has no quarrel with you."

"Unless I miss my guess, this came from Private McCue's uniform." Slocum held out the scrap of cloth.

Gorman and McCue. Slocum had no great liking for either man and knew the feeling was mutual. But he hadn't thought they were crazy enough to ambush him. Or was it Charley they wanted dead? Gorman's irrational hatred of the Walapai might be all that it took for him to order the private to join in on an Indian shoot. It might have been bad luck that Slocum was along with the scout.

Somehow, John Slocum doubted that. The men wanted both him and Charley dead. He remembered the lieutenant's orders too well to think anything else.

"See any sign of Sherum?"

"Not a trace," Charley replied. "My brother's too sneaky for any tracks to be left where we could find them. He's a mite touched in the head, but even Sherum wouldn't drink *this* water." Charley's nose curled at the sulfurous odor hanging in the air.

"Is there better water around?" Slocum asked.

"A few miles back in the direction of the camp," Charley said. "That's why it was so crazy to come here. Sherum wouldn't be here. He might even think to sneak on into the camp at Beale Springs and steal our water." Charley chuckled at such audacity, then hobbled to his horse. Slocum watched and decided the scout might have a bruised leg from the deflected bullet but nothing more.

He clutched the bit of woolen cavalry uniform, then tucked it into his shirt pocket. He had a score to settle with McCue—and Lieutenant Samuel Gorman.

"Out on patrol," Slocum said in disgust. "Gorman and McCue went on a scout and haven't come back yet."

"Know where they went," Charley observed, sitting in the dark outside the troopers' barracks as he honed down what remained of his knife blade into a shorter, more usable weapon. "Might be they heard tell how good sulfur springs were for the body."

"Their health's not going to be their worry when I find them," Slocum said angrily. "They'd better worry about their necks."

"What'd Captain Byrne have to say about the two taking potshots at us?"

"He said he would look into it when he got time. About all he's looking into right now is the mouth of a whiskey bottle."

"Firewater's not much better for him than the sulfur water was for us," Charley said. He held up the two-inch blade and made a face. It wasn't much good for anything after having been struck by the bullet intended for his belly.

"Want some advice?" Slocum asked. Walapai Charley turned toward him, saying nothing.

"Get a new knife. One with a long, sharp blade."

The Indian scout smiled, showing even white teeth. With a flick of his wrist, he sent the short-bladed knife tumbling awkwardly through the air. It sank a half inch into the wood post beside Slocum.

Slocum yanked it free and handed it back to Charley.

"I'll be in Prescott, if anyone wants me," Slocum said. He knew Captain Byrne wouldn't sober up for days, not with the liquor sloshing around in his belly.

"If they come back, I'll let you know right away," Charley said insincerely. Neither the scout nor Slocum thought the pair would return before dawn and possibly not then. They knew their intended victims were not dead—and would be out for blood.

Slocum rode slowly toward Prescott hours away, thinking hard. He'd had no real quarrel with Gorman before now. He hardly expected to find the lieutenant in Prescott but he wanted to be ready for him should their trails cross again. But more than searching for Gorman and McCue, Slocum rode to town to see how Moira Kelson fared.

It was almost four in the morning when he rode into Prescott. The town stirred sluggishly; the saloons and dance halls were still roaring but the rest of the town was quiet. Here and there some milked cows or walked ailing horses but most wouldn't be up for another hour.

He licked dry lips and considered how good a shot of liquor would taste. Somehow, the water in a barrel beside the saloon called more strongly to him. He shoved his head in the rain barrel and let the warm liquid run down his shirt. It wasn't much of a bath but it invigorated him.

Looking around, he homed in on the hotel across the street as if someone called to him. A smile crossed Slocum's face now. That was the kind of place Moira might stay on her way to . . . where?

He led his horse to the trough in front of the hotel, then

went inside. The desk clerk slept, head resting on his crossed arms. Slocum pried loose the guest register without disturbing the man's loud snoring.

"Room two twenty-three," he said, finding Moira's name on the register. He went up the stairs, stepping carefully to avoid any ruckus that might awaken light-sleeping patrons. Stopping in front of the redhead's room, he wondered what the hell he was doing here. He started to knock, then stopped.

Would she even want to see him? They had been thrown together under unusual circumstances. He had rescued her and Monty Kelson, but he had also been there when the Walapai killed her brother. Would she blame him for not doing more, now that she had time to sit and ponder all that had happened to her?

Slocum didn't knock. He reached down and gently tried the doorknob. It turned. Moira had not locked her room before retiring. Or was something wrong? Slocum opened the door and peered in, just to be sure she was all right.

He caught his breath when he saw her on the bed, the bed-clothes draping her slender form. Faint light from outside filtered in through the dirty windowpane in the room, giving the lovely woman an angelic appearance. Slocum started to close the door when Moira stirred.

She moaned softly, turned and pushed away the sheet covering her. She slept buck naked. Slocum saw the creamy white swell of one breast and the dark nub capping it. Her waist was small, and the flare of her hips and buttocks caused Slocum to pause longer than he needed. He ought not spy on her like this, yet he found himself frozen to the spot.

"John," she called out. "John?" Moira pulled a feather pillow close to her, squeezing it hard.

"I'm here, Moira," he said softly. Slocum jumped in surprise when the woman let out a yelp and sat upright in the bed. Her emerald eyes were wide with astonishment and she clutched at the sheet, pulling it up to hide her nakedness.

"What, how, I mean, it's you, isn't it, John?"

"Yes," he said, confused. "You called out my name and I thought you were awake. I didn't mean to—"

"I was dreaming. I didn't think you—" She smoothed her hair, then said, "Come in, quickly now. Don't disturb anyone else." Moira had been chastely hiding herself before. Not now. She wantonly dropped the sheet and exposed all her virtues to him with a boldness Slocum usually saw only in harlots.

But this ravishing creature was no woman of easy virtue, no pretty waiter girl or dance hall whore.

Slocum closed the door behind him, still not sure what to do or where to look without getting embarrassed. He felt like an intruder—until Moira held out her arms to him.

"Come to bed, John. I want you," she said plainly. She licked her lips and pushed away the rest of the covering, in case her invitation might have been misconstrued.

He unbuckled his gun belt and kicked off his boots before dropping to the side of the bed. Moira's eager fingers worked to get him out of his shirt and pants. And then she found other things to keep those fingers busy. Slocum sucked in a breath as her hand closed around his slowly growing manhood.

"Look what I found," she said. "You're surely glad to see me. As glad as I am to see you." With her unoccupied hand, she caught his wrist and pulled his fingers to the fleecy patch between her milky-white thighs.

Slocum rubbed over the furry triangle and then thrust a finger into her moist depths. Moira let out a soft sigh and sank back to the bed. She never let loose of her erotic hold on him and she made sure his finger did not leave its berth. He began stroking it in and out of her slowly. Her slick juices seemed to boil from inside as her arousal grew.

"More, John, I want more than just your finger."

He did not move his hand. Rather, he bent over and lightly kissed the nearest nipple. The coppery, hard nubbin of flesh pulsed with every beat of her heart. As he toyed with the nipple, he felt more and more blood pounding into it. She was getting more excited—and so was he.

Slocum tried to hold back the tensions in his loins that threatened to make him lose all control. Her hand stroked slowly up and down his meaty stalk, every light touch or quick movement pushing him that much closer to acting like a young buck with his first woman.

He left one breast and gave the same attention to the other. Moira's chest heaved up and down. He licked and teased her silky skin as she moved under him, his lips and tongue missing nothing. He found the hollow of her throat and kissed there. Then he moved around slowly, to her shoulders and the nape of her neck. Every kiss there sent a delicious tremor through her.

"Yes, John, so nice. Now make it perfect. Make it the best ever!"

She threw her arms around his neck and pulled him down. Their mouths crushed together as Slocum positioned himself between her parted thighs. As his lust-slickened hand left her most intimate region, he levered his hips forward. The tip of his shaft parted the red-haired vixen's nether lips and plunged fully into her body.

Moira arched her back and ground her crotch into his. She moaned and sobbed and began bucking like a bronco. He held on by cupping her rounded buttocks with his hands. He lifted her up and kept her firmly pressed into his body until he wanted to explode like a stick of dynamite. Only when he thought he could not contain himself any more did he lower her to the bed and withdraw.

"Fast, John, and hard. I want every inch of your wondrous hardness within me." She stroked over his arms and down his flanks, fingertips tracing over the wounds he had received in the past weeks. Every touch spurred him on with a vigor he had seldom experienced.

He slid in and then began stroking with the ages-old rhythm of a man pleasuring a woman. Moira gasped and moaned and a thin sheen of sweat covered her luscious body. Slocum dipped down now and again to lick and nip at her breast, but the tensions he felt in his groin had reached the point of no return.

Just as he muttered, "Can't hold on anymore," he felt her body tense. She shuddered hard all over and a red flush rose from her breasts to her neck as she experienced the same intensity of passion that racked Slocum's body.

Together they strove and then sank exhausted to the bed. Tangled in each other's arms, they said nothing. There was no need. Slocum stared into Moira's green eyes and sank away without a trace. He felt he could lie here forever and not move a muscle. To do so would break the mood.

Unexpectedly, Moira sneezed and pushed back to stifle another. She rubbed her nose and smiled sheepishly.

"I don't know what is in this Arizona dust that makes me sneeze so. It is unladylike to have a running nose the way I do."

"I'd say what you did was very unladylike," Slocum pointed out. "And you didn't hear me complain once."

"Not once," she admitted, "but perhaps I have something to complain about?"

"What?"

"This seems to have gone to sleep." She stroked over his flaccid organ. "I wanted more."

"Greedy," he said. The sudden change of expression on her face told him he had said the wrong thing. "What's the matter? I didn't mean that you were—"

"It's nothing you said, John. It got me to thinking about

how awful things are at the cavalry post at Beale Springs."

Slocum pulled the pillow around and fluffed it up so they could lie side by side on it. Moira leaned back, staring up at the whitewashed ceiling ten feet above.

"I wasn't long at the camp but it is obvious Captain Byrne is a drunkard. Not that there is anything wrong in that, mind you," she said. "More than one Irishman has been known to take a nip, but the captain is letting his liquor fog his judgment."

This was nothing Slocum had not heard before—or seen for himself. He remained quiet as Moira rattled on with a litany of problems she saw.

"He has lost control of his men, and the problem with feeding the Walapai under the treaty are sorely straining the camp's resources."

"How's that?" Slocum had to ask. He reached over and played with a conveniently naked nipple. Moira seemed not to notice his attentions. She was too busy detailing what she had seen.

"The men at the post have been selling the surplus food on the black market. Now that the Indians are claiming their share, there's no more to go around. This has put a crimp in many a man's finances."

"Like McCue and Gorman," Slocum said. He had thought as much. It had to be true if even a casual observer like Moira Kelson noticed.

"Those are two of the ones," Moira said. "But they are not the only thieves. I heard several talking among themselves, expressing real discontent with the treaty. They want Sherum to succeed so all the Walapai go on the warpath again."

"I can see Gorman doing all he can to sabotage the treaty," Slocum agreed.

"He's a sorry case, now isn't he?" Moira asked. "His entire family killed the way they were and all."

"I hadn't heard this." Slocum pushed himself up a bit in bed. His hand left Moira's breast. She trapped his brawny wrist and pulled it back. He smiled a little but his own thoughts turned to Samuel Gorman rather than spending a few more pleasant hours with Moira.

"His wife and two sons were on their way from Kansas City to join him at Fort Whipple. They were on a government wagon train somewhere to the east, some spot I have ne'er heard of before. Fort Wingate, perhaps."

"Up in Navajo country," Slocum said.

"Perhaps so. The wagon train was attacked and only a few survived."

"Weren't Walapai doing the attacking," Slocum said. "Might not have been the Navajo, either. Who can tell? A Ute raiding party from up north or Arapaho. Even Comanches wander that far west on occasion."

"He blames all Indians for his loss, he does," Moira said. "A sad thing, but it has filled him with bitterness."

"And greed," Slocum said, "if he is dipping into McCue's racket of peddling food on the black market. The supply master puts in requisitions for half again as much as is needed to maintain a post. Most of the overage is written off as spoiled— and it usually is."

"I tasted some of their meat." Moira spat in a very unlady-like fashion. "The only real meat in it were the maggots."

Slocum swung out of the bed, scratched himself and went to the window. The sun rose, casting bright beams of light through the window. When he had ridden into Prescott the town had been somnolent. Now it bustled with early-morning activity. He listened to Moira with half an ear as he studied the streets.

The blue of a cavalry trooper's uniform caught his eye. Wiping away some of the grime on the window, he pressed his face into the glass.

"It's McCue!" he cried. "I'll be back."

Before Moira could protest, Slocum struggled to pull on his pants and boots. He had his shirt on as he reached the hall outside her room. He strapped on his gun belt as he hurried down the stairs and finished buttoning his shirt by the time he hit the streets. He was dressed, and he was spoiling for a fight.

In the middle of Prescott's main street, Slocum called in a loud voice, "McCue! We have a score to settle!"

The rush of commerce in Prescott fell to a deathly silence as citizens began ducking inside. No one wanted to be an easy target when the bullets started flying.

11

"I know what you've been doing, McCue," called Slocum, stance wide and ready. He would have drawn and fired on the bushwhacking private if he hadn't seen the man was unarmed. McCue had been drinking and might have bartered his sidearm for another round. Or he might have been lucky enough to have forgotten it back at camp.

"What's that?" McCue's words slurred. He stumbled along the street, one eye closed to give a better focus. "You!" When McCue recognized Slocum he sobered fast.

"Unless I miss my guess, this will fit the hole in your uniform," Slocum said, holding out the torn patch he had found where McCue had tried to drygulch him. "Was it off an arm? Your left arm?"

The way McCue guiltily checked that arm and found a hole told Slocum all he needed to know.

"You've been selling the surplus food at the Beale Springs camp on the black market. Giving the excess to the Walapai put a crimp in your scheme, didn't it?''

"What are you going on about, Slocum? You drunk?''

"Sober. And you're going to be dead, you bushwhacking son of a bitch.''

"I ain't armed. You wouldn't kill an unarmed man.''

"You tried to shoot me in the back. You don't deserve any better than a coiled rattler,'' Slocum said, but his hot anger now became something more deadly. Coldness filled him, and he knew he would not draw his Colt Navy. He strode forward.

For a moment, McCue thought to make a stand. Then he saw the hardness in Slocum's eyes. He turned to run, only to fall over himself in his headlong retreat. Slocum reached him in a flash.

Jerking the private to his feet, Slocum reared back and unloaded a powerful blow to the man's belly. McCue grunted and went to one knee. On the way down, Slocum lifted a knee into McCue's chin. Then he began to whale the tar out of him.

"Stop, stop it. He didn't do nuthin' to you!'' Hands grabbed at Slocum to keep him from hammering McCue to the ground. Slocum pushed free for a moment and got in another punch to McCue's face. Pain shot all the way up Slocum's arm to his shoulder. The pain of fist against bony face brought him up short and let the gathering crowd pull him back.

"He busted my nose. He tried to beat me to death!'' moaned McCue. Blood spurting from the deformed nose made the damage look far worse than it was. Slocum wished he had been able to continue punching at McCue for another few minutes. Then the disfigurement would have matched the flood of red blood.

"He tried to gun me down north of Beale Springs,'' Slocum said. "He tried to kill another scout from the camp, too.''

"Walapai Charley's only an Injun,'' whined McCue. "He don't count. And this one's been eatin' loco weed. He's plumb crazy.''

Strong grips held Slocum back as he surged forward again.

"I'm gonna run you in if you don't cool that hot head of yours," came the marshal's warning. "I don't rightly know what sparked this row, and I don't want to know. When you gents are in Prescott, you obey the law. If this has something to do with cavalry matters, take it up with Captain Byrne."

"A good idea," Slocum said, wondering if Byrne had sobered yet. He doubted it from the amount of liquor the camp commander had downed. The empty bottles formed a small cairn outside his office at the camp.

He glanced around the tight knot of spectators and saw more than one blue uniform. The cavalry troopers' faces told him he was not well thought of at the moment. Were they all getting a cut of McCue and Gorman's scheme? Slocum doubted it. More than likely, they sided with their comrade against what they saw as a crazy scout.

"I want Byrne to hear what I have to say—if he's not drinking his fool head off again." This brought a few murmurs from the soldiers. They knew their commander's penchant for drink as well as Slocum. But having it brought to the attention of the Prescott citizens didn't set well with them, either.

This was a family dispute, as they saw it, and Slocum was out of line even mentioning it in public.

"Get on back to your camp 'fore I run the lot of you in," the marshal said. Slocum knew the man wasn't bluffing by the way deputies moved through the crowd. If the marshal gave the high sign, those deputies could have half the soldiers on the ground and the other half covered in a split second.

"Let's ride on back—and don't try to leave my sight," Slocum warned. He rested his hand on his six-shooter.

"Hey now, I tole you, none of that in Prescott." The marshal waved, and the deputies began to disperse the crowd. In less than a minute all the locals were gone, leaving only blue-uniformed troopers. Slocum hunted for any of the men he had ridden with. Even Corporal Framingham would have been a friendly face, but none of these men had ridden recently enough with Slocum to back him in a fight with McCue.

As he mounted his horse, Slocum saw Moira Kelson in the hotel window. He touched the brim of his battered, floppy black hat in acknowledgment, then wheeled about and rode off to keep up with Private McCue. The surly enlisted man rode at a breakneck pace, as if he could lose Slocum this way. Slocum kept up easily enough until they were in sight of the camp. Then McCue slowed, as if realizing he might lose in a dispute brought before Captain Byrne.

"We kin work this out, Slocum," McCue said. "Let bygones be bygones."

Slocum reached over and grabbed the man's arm and tugged. The torn spot on his left sleeve matched the scrap of fabric Slocum carried in his shirt pocket. He released McCue and said nothing. The private realized trying to kill Slocum had been a bad idea.

And even worse, was not succeeding.

They rode into the parade ground, and Slocum immediately saw that bringing charges against McCue would do him no more good now than they would have the night before. Thomas Byrne had added at least one more quart whiskey bottle to the pile outside his quarters.

The captain sat in front of his office, singing off-key. Slocum had never heard this particular bawdy song before and wasn't inclined to stand around listening.

McCue's attitude turned swiftly, like a cutting horse. He had been willing to apologize and curry favor seconds earlier. Now he saw Byrne's condition and cried, "Looks as if Gorman's in command right now. You want to complain to him, Slocum?"

Slocum's fingers tapped lightly on the ebony handle of his Colt Navy. McCue blanched at the motion and tried to back away. He almost fell from his horse. Slocum said nothing as he turned his pony's face and headed for the corral. He had put fear into McCue but this would come back to haunt him, he knew. Men like McCue were backshooters. Now that he was spooked, he would fight like a cornered rat.

He would have to watch every step from now on.

The afternoon came and went, Slocum biding his time. McCue didn't show, so Slocum tended his chores. Currying his horse just before sundown, Slocum heard soft footsteps approaching from behind. He didn't bother turning.

"You should be more careful," came a familiar voice.

"I knew it was you, Charley," Slocum said, continuing to groom his horse. "You walk light. If it had been McCue or Gorman, there would have been more noise than a mad badger in a burlap bag."

Walapai Charley chuckled and perched on the top rail of the corral fence.

"You don't make many friends with your ways, Slocum," the scout said.

Slocum shrugged. He had been told that before. And it didn't bother him. Making friends with a sidewinder was a good way to get bit when he least expected it—and it wouldn't be the sidewinder's fault. A snake was a snake by nature. It would be his fault if he ever forgot that.

"I shouldn't be talking to you, either."

"Afraid to be seen with me?" This struck Slocum as funny.

"There's gettin' to be more of the troopers willin' to plug an Indian, any Indian. You be seen with me too much, and they'll bury us both in the same grave."

"I could have worse company," Slocum allowed. He finished with his horse and swung up to sit beside Charley. "Has Byrne sobered up for more than ten minutes in the past twenty-four hours?"

Charley shook his head.

Slocum held his tongue. Walking toward them on unsteady feet was the camp commander. Captain Byrne saw them and lengthened his stride. Somehow, he kept from falling over.

"You two, I want a word with you."

"Want more 'n that with you," Charley said under his breath.

"If it's about Private McCue, I want to—"

"How'd you hear?" Byrne's eyes went wide. Slocum saw the bloodshot tracks that looked like a bear had clawed the captain's eyeballs. "I only got the report a few minutes ago."

"He tried to drygulch Charley and me," Slocum said.

"I know nothing of this. McCue and five others have deserted."

"Does it have something to do with them selling the surplus food from the post sutler?" asked Slocum.

Byrne gaped and nodded. Slocum read the consternation on the captain's face as if it had been the headlines of a newspaper. Byrne was wondering how he was the last to hear of the thievery and black marketeering.

"McCue's gone and I want to find him," Byrne said. "This is bad for morale, this desertion. Taking five others with him is intolerable."

"Did Gorman hightail it, too?" asked Charley.

"Lieutenant Gorman? Of course not. Why should he? Without Gorman, this post would be in far worse shape than it is. A good officer, a good man. I could use a dozen more like him."

Slocum and Walapai Charley exchanged silent looks. It would do no good now to report their suspicions to the camp commander. They knew McCue had been one of their ambushers. They only suspected Gorman. But Slocum wasn't going to turn his back on the lieutenant, not for an instant.

"You want us to track down McCue and bring him back?"

"Keep this mission a secret, Slocum," cautioned Byrne.

"Bad for morale, very bad." He licked his lips and patted himself down, searching for a flask. He came up dry. "Charley, go to Chief Levy-Levy and ask for a few of his best trackers to accompany us. We will furnish the supplies. Then all of us will go after McCue and the others and return them for immediate trial."

Walapai Charley dropped from the rail and walked off, never looking back. Slocum wondered what thoughts ran through the scout's head. He wasn't even sure what he thought about this manhunt.

"You coming with us, Captain?" he asked finally.

"I am. It is my duty to be sure no disturbance wrecks morale at the camp."

"You leaving Gorman in charge while we're gone?" asked Slocum.

"Of course. He is a good officer, one of the best in my command." Byrne frowned at this, as if his brain wanted to explode from so much thinking.

Slocum considered simply riding off. Moira waited back in Prescott, but he didn't know how long she would stay. There hadn't been time for a decent farewell, not after he spotted McCue from her hotel window. But riding with Byrne was better than remaining at Beale Springs. Leaving Gorman in command at Beale Springs was like putting the fox in charge of the henhouse.

"McCue didn't strike me as a good trailsman," Slocum said. "We can find him pretty quick."

"Good, good. I must saddle now and prepare. We leave in a half hour, Slocum." Captain Byrne marched off in the direction of the small barn and storage area. As he walked his stride firmed and he didn't wobble as much. The alcoholic haze was lifting from his brain. Slocum hoped it would continue.

12

"They don't cover their trail," Walapai Charley observed. He knelt on the road and ran his fingers around the hoofprints of the horses the deserters had stolen. "This one's shoe is cracked. Needs replacing or the horse will pull up lame."

"I checked supplies and they didn't bother taking any spare horseshoes," Slocum said. He rubbed his stubbled chin and brushed dust off his hat. He squinted into the sunlight. They had been on the deserters' trail two days now. Unlike following—or trying to follow Sherum—the trail was plain enough for a blind man to follow.

Slocum smiled wryly at the notion. It was plain enough even for Captain Byrne to follow when he was blind drunk. The officer had been fighting to keep his hand out of the sloshing saddlebags dangling behind him, but now and then his resolve faded and his thirst overtook him.

At the moment, Byrne was sober enough. He argued with the four Walapai scouts Chief Levy-Levy had sent along. Slocum counted that as something of a coup for the cavalry officer. If he had ordered out a company of his own men, he would have had dozens more deserters by now. The Walapai had nowhere else to go.

"They make good time," Charley said. "They don't stop to hunt or find food. How long can their provisions last?"

"How long can their water last?" Slocum countered. Even with two canteens apiece, the fleeing men had to find water soon.

"They are heading into the Black Mountains," said Charley, standing and squinting into the sun. "There's no good way across to get to the Colorado River, except Union Pass. It lies in that direction." Charley pointed due west, at an angle to the road.

"If we head directly there, you think we can head them off?"

Charley nodded. "They rely on speed to escape, nothing more." He tapped the side of his head. "If they knew where they ran and went directly, we would not stand a chance of catching them."

"But they're following the road," Slocum finished. "That means we can get to Union Pass before them."

"Possibly." Charley swung into the saddle, favoring his hip. Slocum wondered if the scout had allowed Doc Gavilan to examine him after McCue's bullet had struck him. He doubted it. None of the Walapai had much truck with the camp doctor.

Slocum scratched at his own healing wounds and knew the reason. Gavilan did little to inspire confidence in white men, much less Indians used to a different brand of healing. Slocum wished he had asked Charley which medicine man had fixed him up. Charley might be farther along than he was in mending.

"Captain," called Slocum. "We're striking out across

country, going directly to Union Pass. We think McCue and the others are headed there.''

Byrne spoke briefly with one of Levy-Levy's men, then motioned for Slocum to lead the way.

"They're getting real chummy," Slocum said as he and Charley rode side by side. "I wouldn't have thought Byrne would cozy up to Levy-Levy's men the way he's doing."

"It's the firewater," Charley said. "They all share a common hobby." The scout spat and put his heels to his horse's flanks and left Slocum behind. Slocum tugged on his reins and rode off at an angle, intending to go out a mile and then angle back to the line of travel taken by Byrne and the Walapai scouts. This would give him the lay of the land and assure him they weren't riding into a trap.

He discounted McCue and the others bushwhacking them. But Chief Sherum had been raiding with impunity. Two more stagecoaches had been held up, all the passengers in one killed. No reports from the hills around Beale Springs had come in reporting more miners slaughtered, but Slocum figured that was due to Sherum's efficiency. He killed everyone who might bring the account of new depredation to the cavalry.

Slocum rejoined Byrne and the others two hours past sunset. Union Pass lay more than ten miles away, but he worried about traveling in the dark.

"We camp," Byrne decided. "We can reach the pass by midday. McCue and the others won't have reached it by then, will they, Slocum?"

Slocum shook his head. He had no way of knowing how desperate McCue was.

"Good. We camp and ride at first light." Byrne prepared his bedroll and sank down, asleep in minutes. Slocum's belly grumbled. He needed food more than sleep right now, but what he itched for most of all was Private McCue in his gun sight.

"You want to keep moving?" he asked Walapai Charley. The scout pursed his lips, looked at the Walapai with Byrne and finally heaved a deep sigh.

"Won't do any good."

"You don't get along too good with them, do you?" Slocum asked.

"They know I'm Sherum's half brother. And that I've scouted for the cavalry too long. I'm not Indian, I'm not white eyes. They ignore me because I don't fit into their world all nice and neat."

"It happens," Slocum said. "I move on when I get that feeling."

Charley laughed. "And where does an Indian go? This is my land, what the government is willing to give back to me. If I leave, I leave all I have known. And if I stay, my own people think I am a traitor."

"You could always join Sherum," Slocum opined.

Charley spat and then laughed harshly. "No way. He enjoys killing. He might settle down if we make it plain he cannot win. But Sherum will always be trouble. It will take more than Captain Thomas Byrne to pacify that renegade."

Slocum thought Charley sounded a little envious of his half brother but said nothing more. He pried open a can of peaches and worked at some of the trail biscuits he had brought along. Hunting a rabbit would have suited him more, but getting down from the horse produced a curious lethargy in him. He was too tired to go hunting with only a knife, and a rifle shot might bring unwanted guests.

This was Sherum's country. The wily chief might pop up anytime, anywhere. He lay down after burying his empty can and was asleep within minutes.

A little before dawn, Slocum rose and tended his horse. By

this time the others were up and about, ready for the hard ride directly into Union Pass. For some reason Charley only grunted when Slocum spoke to him. He let the scout ride alone, wrapped in his own dark thoughts as they searched for McCue's trail.

They found it just before noon.

"The deserters beat us to the pass," Slocum said, his keen eyes working over the tracks on the dusty road. "There's the horse with the cracked shoe. I recognize a couple others, too."

"Horse is going lame. Be easy to capture them in another day. Less," said Charley.

"They cannot get ahead of us!" cried Byrne. He worked to control his high-spirited horse. Slocum had to give the officer his due. Byrne had not been tippling too much and seemed the field commander he had been when Slocum had reported to Fort Whipple seven months back.

"No sense killing our horses," Slocum pointed out. "The pass funnels them through to the far side. We can—"

"Once they reach the Colorado River, they can go in either direction. We will never know. Even the sloppiest of frontiersman can hide from us."

"So we split up when we reach the river, Captain," Slocum said. "That way, one group of us is sure to find them—or maybe both groups. What works for them also works against them."

"What do you mean, Slocum?" Byrne peered at Slocum hard.

"They aren't going to get out of the canyon easily. They have to go either up or downstream. They don't have any other choice. We've closed the gap between us. Another day will see us on top of them."

"They might not know we are close," cut in Charley. "They put too much faith in speed instead of guile."

"Well, yes, that might be. Come along now. We waste precious minutes. I will not tolerate any deserters from my unit. They will pay to the full extent allowed by military justice, each of them!'' Byrne lifted his arm and made a grand sweeping gesture, as if he commanded a battalion instead of a ragtag band of Walapai scouts.

Slocum and Charley trotted forward and led through Union Pass. As he rode, Slocum kept craning his neck around, peering at the bluffs on either side of the path. He remembered how Sherum had almost killed him in a similar canyon. The differences this time were telling, though. From far ahead Slocum heard the mighty rush of the Colorado River—and no Walapai braves sought his scalp, either from ambush along the road or from the towering cliffs.

"There," said Charley as they reached an overlook to the river. "They are *there*." He stabbed his finger in the direction of the white-capped waters.

For a moment Slocum thought he spoke in a general sense, then saw the group of six men on the nearer bank of the river. A slow smile crossed his lips.

"We have them," he agreed. "They can't be more than twenty minutes ahead of us." He picked out the trail leading down and knew he could overtake McCue and the others in even less time.

Captain Byrne and the Walapai scouts reined in and watched as McCue and the deserters dismounted and allowed their horses to drink from the river.

"Can we approach without spooking them? I want to take them all as quickly as possible." Byrne's decisiveness told Slocum the captain had not been hitting the bottle. Somehow, being in the field invigorated him and turned him away from the bottle.

"The track down is exposed," Slocum said, estimating how long it would take to reach the banks of the Colorado River.

"We can't sneak down on them. Better would be to rush them."

"Our horses would tire before we got halfway," Charley protested. "Let them choose how to proceed, either upstream or down. We follow in an hour and capture them when they camp."

"We go all-out now," Byrne decided.

The Walapai with him let out whoops and galloped off, kicking up a huge dust cloud on the winding road leading down to the river. This wasn't what Slocum had considered when he suggested rushing the deserters. They might have gotten halfway down to the river before being sighted if they had proceeded quietly but quickly. Not now.

The Walapai scouts spooked the deserters.

"They're splitting into two groups," Slocum shouted. "You follow the ones going upstream. Charley and I will take the pair running downstream."

Captain Byrne acknowledged with a gesture, then put his heels into his horse and charged after Levy-Levy's men.

"This might take longer than I thought," Charley said.

"You were right," Slocum admitted. "We ought to have waited."

Charley shook his head. "Too quick to rush in, too quick to die."

"They don't have to lay a trap for us, not this time," Slocum said. "They're running, and we're hot on their heels."

Charley let out a snort and urged his horse forward into a canter, Slocum a few yards behind and eating the scout's dust. They reached the Colorado River only to find Byrne and the others had pursued those going to the north and east.

"Two, only two in this direction," Charley said from the ground. He ran his finger around the muddy track already filling with water. "The cracked shoe is on one horse. We have the easy chase. Already the horse goes lame."

Slocum and Walapai Charley set off with the Colorado River at their right, wary of any trap set for them in the winding canyon. They need not have worried. The two deserters they tracked sought only escape. And in less than fifteen minutes, Slocum spotted one blue-clad man working frantically on his horse's back hoof.

"Threw a shoe," Charley said. "We have that one."

"And the other. He stayed with his friend."

"Good. They can be captured together and save us much trouble." Charley slid from the saddle and grabbed his rifle. Slocum unsheathed his Winchester and levered a round into the chamber. He waited for Charley to take to the rocks and get into position higher on the canyon wall before riding forward.

"Give up. We've got you, fair and square," Slocum shouted. Disappointed neither of the men was John McCue, Slocum wanted only to capture them and get on the private's trail.

"You aren't takin' us back!" shouted one. He lifted his carbine and got off a shot. Slocum worked to control his paint. The shot had missed by a country mile, but the young buck might get lucky.

"Don't try it!" Slocum shouted. He did not worry about the man's second shot. Walapai Charley was too good a shot. The trooper yelped and clawed at his side where the scout's bullet had creased him.

The other trooper, trying to keep his lame horse from limping off, realized there was no escape. Slowly raising his hands, he called, "Don't shoot! I give up!"

From the canyon wall came Charley, his rifle ready if either man tried to make a run for it. Slocum rode closer, keeping them covered, also. All the fight had gone out of the pair.

"Put these on them," Slocum said, tossing Charley a set of manacles. "That will keep them from wandering off again."

Slocum jerked his rifle up and sighted along the barrel when the first trooper started to strike Charley. The scout stepped to one side, giving Slocum a better shot. The deserter quieted and accepted the manacles on his wrists with ill grace.

"There'd've been no need to leave if it weren't for the likes of you," he shouted at Slocum.

"What do you mean?"

"You and that Injun-loving captain of ours. Byrne never saw an Indian he didn't like. We ought to be fighting them all, not just Sherum."

"Chief Levy-Levy signed the treaty," Charley said in a level voice. "What more can you want?"

"To kill every last one of you!"

"Reckon these gents were getting a share of the food now going to Levy-Levy's clan," Slocum said. From the dark looks he got from both men, he knew this was true. Too many troopers supplemented their pitiful wages with black marketeering.

"How else could we live?" asked the trooper with the lame horse. "We got an Indian-loving commander who hasn't done near enough to stop Sherum. And he's giving away *our* supplies. That food goes straight to Sherum's men."

"You saying Levy-Levy is giving the food to Sherum?" Slocum wanted to laugh. From all he had heard, Sherum had no greater enemy than Levy-Levy. Chief Levy-Levy's authority had been questioned and his tribe split apart by the hotheaded Sherum. Levy-Levy had chosen peace and Sherum the warpath. For one to supply the other was crazy.

"What else? McCue said it was so. We're gettin' killed on patrol because we're keepin' Sherum alive with our own food. Wouldn't put it past Byrne to be givin' them redskins ammunition and arms, too!"

"You spend too much time listening to McCue and not enough time thinking for yourself," Slocum said. "Get on.

Both of you on the one horse.''

Slowly, they made their way back to the road coming across Union Pass. They reached it an hour past sunset.

"You want to see our guests back to Camp Beale Springs and let me join Byrne and the others?''

"You want McCue real bad, don't you?'' asked Charley. "Ever think I might not want to take a cut or two at him myself?''

Slocum champed at the bit. They had caught two deserters, but four were still on the loose upstream. He was a mite surprised Byrne and Levy-Levy's scouts had not bagged their quarry by now.

"Slocum. Listen hard.'' Charley cocked his head to one side.

Slocum turned slowly until he heard what Charley already had. The steady click-click of shod hooves against rock told of an approaching party from upstream.

"Byrne?''

Walapai Charley said nothing. There was no way to tell. But the horses were shod. Slocum couldn't rule out the chance it was McCue, though how the private could have successfully ambushed Byrne and the Walapai scouts was beyond him.

"Slocum!'' came the greeting. Captain Byrne rode up, trailed by the Walapai.

"Captain, you find McCue and the others?''

"We did,'' Byrne said. He almost hiccuped. From the way he fought to sit erect, his saddlebags rode quite a few ounces of whiskey lighter than when he had set out after the deserters.

"And?'' Slocum's fingers tapped nervously on the butt of his six-shooter. He didn't like this, not one bit.

"McCue tried to escape arrest, as did the o-others. They will not be st-standing trial for their desertion.''

Slocum was startled that Byrne had killed the four fleeing troopers but said nothing. The cavalry officer had already turned his horse up the steep trail leading through Union Pass and back to Camp Beale Springs.

Charley and Slocum brought up the rear of the party, their two prisoners riding in frightened silence.

13

"There's no way we can keep up with Sherum," Slocum told Captain Byrne. "He moves too fast. He knows the territory better than anybody here, except Levy-Levy's scouts."

"Then we must recruit them for hunting down Sherum," Byrne said decisively. Slocum wondered if this might be braggadocio bubbling up from the immense amounts of whiskey the captain had drunk the past week since they had brought back two of the six deserters, or if Byrne had sobered enough to have a real opinion.

When the Camp Beale Springs commander was sober, there was none better. But the pressures of garrison command wore on him. Slocum had heard that the daily telegrams from Washington delivered to the commander's desk spoke of discipline if he did not bring Sherum to bay quickly. Those were the words of bureaucrats hiding away two thousand miles off, men who could never know the danger and difficulty of finding a man as clever as Sherum.

"There might be another way," Slocum said.

"A moment," Byrne interrupted. He frowned as he stared out the door of his small office at the angry group of settlers moving in his direction. "I seem to have other matters to tend to at the moment."

Slocum snorted in disgust. Byrne drifted away from the conversation more and more, especially when he was hitting the bottle. Rotgut whiskey tore away huge chunks of the man's good sense and concentration, but this time Byrne might have been right to ignore Slocum in favor of other concerns.

"We want a word with you, Byrne!" shouted the settler's leader, a florid man with a scraggly beard.

"How can I help you?" asked Byrne, stepping outside into the hot sun. "Has Chief Sherum launched an attack against your farms?"

"We come from Hardyville. We ain't sodbusters. We're decent people, merchants and the like. They told us over at Fort Mojave to bring our complaint to you, so here we are."

"What is the nature of this . . . complaint? Hardyville is some distance from here. My men cannot have hurrahed your town, as they have done once or twice in Prescott. We—"

"You're a damned murderer, that's what you are, Thomas Byrne!" shouted a woman with the group. She stepped forward. "I seen him with my own eyes. I thought the murder was done by Injuns, but they was kilt by you and yours!"

"What are you saying?" Byrne wobbled a bit and then supported himself against the post holding up the porch roof to his office.

"We found that one floating in the river. All he had on was his drawers, socks, and part of a shirt. He was shot in the back, Byrne! We found the place where he was kilt and plenty of evidence you done the crime."

Slocum walked to the wagon and pulled back the tarp thrown over the body. His nose wrinkled. John McCue had been floating in the Colorado River for a spell. And sure as the townspeople had claimed, the trooper had been shot in the back. One round had caught him high on the shoulder. The other had busted his spine.

"We found two others so bad broke up by the river we couldn't tell what happened to them. But if this one is any indication, you had them shot in the back, too!"

"Please, you don't understand," Byrne started. Slocum saw Lieutenant Gorman to one side, a smirk on his face. Before Slocum could stop the captain, Byrne blurted out his confession.

"I shot McCue! I had to. He was a deserter fleeing justice."

"He was stripped. The other two didn't have no clothes, neither," said the woman, more outraged than ever. "We got sons in the cavalry, some of us. I don't want my boy shot down like a dog."

"McCue was a deserter. I had no choice but to shoot."

"How'd he come to lose his clothes, Captain?" asked the red-faced shopkeeper, pushing back to the front of the crowd. "Tell us that. All of them were stripped."

"The Walapai with me. I let them take what they wanted. As payment for their fine work." Byrne lurched and caught himself. The sun and the liquor took their toll on him.

"We heard it plain as day. The captain's confessed to murdering this one and letting them savages have their way with the others. We need to get the territorial governor to hear this!"

The Hardyville citizens backed off. One glanced into the rear of the wagon, undecided what to do. Then he whipped the mule hauling the wagon and headed out of the camp, McCue's body still rotting in the back. Slocum doubted the private would see a grave any time soon. That didn't bother him too much. What the people might do to Captain Byrne, using the body as evidence, did.

Chief Sherum was a knife ready to slash all their throats. What Byrne had done was wrong, but bigger troubles faced the citizens of Arizona Territory at the moment, troubles Byrne was capable of solving.

"I dispute your authority in this matter," Byrne said loudly. Slocum watched the commander of Camp Beale Springs hang on to the edge of the table to steady himself. Since the Hardyville citizens had come to the camp, Byrne had drunk more than ever. In spite of the liquor sloshing in his belly, he still presented a decent defense.

So far.

"I am appointed by the Superintendent of Indian Affairs to look into this distasteful matter," Henry Eastman said in a high-pitched voice. The mousy man took off his spectacles and nervously polished them on the bartender's dirty rag. Seeing that he only smeared his eyeglasses worse, Eastman dropped the rag and put the wire-frame glasses back on.

Eastman peered at the stack of papers in front of him, as if reading them for the first time. Slocum knew the man only stalled for time. He had been in town for days interviewing Prescott's citizens, as well as those from Hardyville willing to come and testify against Byrne.

"I am a captain in the United States Cavalry and any charges lodged against me must be ad-adjudicated in a military tribunal," Byrne said, stumbling on the words.

"That does seem to be true, to a point," Eastman said. "Your relations with the Walapai are to be considered. The treaty does not allow them to rob dead soldiers."

"They were deserters," Byrne said.

"Well, yes, of course they were," Eastman said in his squeaky voice. He nervously licked his lips and reached for a shot glass at one side of the table. He took a sip and made a face. Slocum wasn't even sure it held whiskey.

But what else but outright drunkenness would cause Eastman to back down the way he already was? He had not come
out snorting fire and going for Byrne's scalp the way he ought
to have. There could be no disputing the holes in John
McCue's back. Deserter or not, the man had been gunned
down from behind. With the Walapai scouts accompanying
Byrne, McCue would have been an easy capture.

"Tell me what happened, Captain Byrne." The bureaucrat
leaned back and tented his fingers under his chin, as if listening to some fine chamber music playing rather than the tall
tale Byrne had been spinning to anyone who would listen.

Byrne struck a pose as if he were an orator, then launched
into the most outrageous lies Slocum had ever heard. Slocum
got up and left the saloon, going into the heat boiling the
people of Prescott.

"Can't take it any more?"

Slocum shook his head. Walapai Charley had seated himself
near an open window to listen to the proceedings.

"I hear tell men who have too much to drink see visions,"
Charley went on. "The captain might have seen this—in a
vision."

"He surely didn't see it with two sober eyes," Slocum said
in disgust. "That little weasel of a bureaucrat is buying the
story whole hog."

"Will you tell him anything different when you testify?"
asked Charley.

"Wasn't asked," Slocum said glumly. "If I volunteer the
truth, I might as well ride on out—and watch my back every
inch of the way. The men at the camp think I'm in Byrne's
pocket, being all friendly with the Walapai. And the Walapai
scouts wouldn't take kindly to it if I told everyone I think they
are murderers just like Byrne."

"Nowhere to turn," Charley said.

Slocum laughed harshly and said, "You're in a worse crossfire. Byrne doesn't like you and none of the soldiers do, either. Your own people think you have sold out.''

"Not all of them. Just Sherum,'' said Walapai Charley. "Maybe Levy-Levy, too, but I haven't talked to him. This is bad business, killing McCue and the others, then letting the scouts strip them. Byrne should have paid them enough not to take valuables from the bodies.''

"It's done in battle all the time. But this is different,'' Slocum said. "It's outright robbery if you shoot your victim in the back.''

"Dead is dead. Does McCue care?'' asked Charley.

Slocum cared. He didn't cotton much to riding with a man who would gun down another he had been entrusted to bring back alive. No matter what fiction Byrne spun for Henry Eastman, there had been no reason to cut down McCue from behind. The private and the others running with him had not been good enough frontiersmen to put up any real fight. The ease with which Slocum and Charley had caught the other pair proved that.

"Byrne's not even mentioning that McCue was stealing from the Walapai rations. It's as if your people don't even exist,'' Slocum said in disgust.

Charley laughed at this. He spat, wiped his lips, and thought for a minute.

"They care about Sherum. Maybe I can do something to get my brother talking. Then they would care about me. I could bring about peace.''

"Just don't get caught in the middle. That's where the most bullets are,'' Slocum said, turning from the circus playing out inside the saloon. Byrne warmed to his lies and had an appreciative audience for stories about his personal bravery and how John McCue really had to be shot in the back as he tried to escape custody.

Slocum went across the street and down a few blocks to the

hotel. He wondered if Moira had left already. Events had kept him from even checking the register to see if she had left Prescott. He hoped she had not. The sudden departure when he had gone after McCue had left too many loose ends for his liking.

He opened the door and bumped into someone coming out.

"Excuse me, ma'am," he said. Then he recognized Moira.

"John!" Her lovely pale face lit up like the very sun. "I wondered what had happened to you after that fight in the street. I asked around and all I could find out was that you had returned straightaway to Beale Springs."

"It got complicated real quick. You hear about Byrne shooting McCue in the back?"

A shadow fluttered over her loveliness. She pursed her lips and nodded.

"A terrible thing. Were you involved?"

"Charley and I caught two of the men. Byrne murdered the rest." Slocum felt his ire rising again and didn't like it. He wanted nothing to poison the time he had with Moira. Somehow, he thought it would be too brief.

"I'm surprised to still find you in town. I came over first chance to see if you had left. I'm glad to see you haven't moved on."

"Take me to lunch. I am famished." She held out her arm. He took it and they went back into the street. The only times he had eaten in Prescott had been in saloons, and he wasn't going to follow her brother and his partner's lead in taking her into any drinking establishment. Ladies did not enter such places.

"There's a place that looks decent," Slocum said, seeing a small café crushed between a bookstore and a women's clothing shop.

"I had intended to leave after you ran out as you did on me," she said as they entered. "Business matters kept me here. Business and . . . unfinished business.''

"The mine?" Slocum guessed. He knew what the unfinished business she referred to was, also. He felt the same way.
They had parted too hurriedly, no matter that the hours before
had been so pleasantly spent.

"I find it difficult to sell the mine. Although I am Monty's
only kin and Sean had no family, title cannot pass directly to
me because of my sex.''

"There are ways to get around that. Any banker can sell
the mine for you, pass the money through their hands after
taking some for themselves, and then give you what's left.''

"I discovered that their share is outrageously high. It seems
no one wants to buy mining property at the moment, either.''
Moira stiffened as she spoke and Slocum knew the cause.

"Chief Sherum," Slocum said with some bitterness. "He's
been killing miners, and anyone riding a stagecoach between
Fort Mojave and Prescott is in real danger. That would hold
down interest in buying a mine.''

"I fear the Three Card Monte is less than a spectacular
property. Monty and Sean made a living from it, but not a
good one.''

"It's all you have?" Slocum read the answer on Moira's
lovely face. It might amount to only a few greenbacks but it
was her brother's legacy. That counted more than wealth with
her.

"Will you help me sell the mine, John? I would rather give
you the middleman's fee than some portly banker. You know
mining. I could tell by the way you fixed those sticks of dynamite.''

"I've some acquaintance with mining," Slocum allowed.
"But I can't take the time to find a buyer for the mine. Could
take weeks. Mostly it depends on stopping Sherum and re-
storing some peace to the territory. Until then, no one will
touch that mine with a ten-foot pole.''

"I'm not looking to become rich. I just don't want to be cheated and, John, I don't trust anyone else in this matter. I know I can count on you, as I have in the past."

She took his hand and held it. He stared into her green eyes and wondered what the hell he was going to do. He wasn't a land broker, and he certainly wasn't a magician who could summon up solutions to all the troubles plaguing Moira Kelson and the Arizona Territory.

14

"You already know. Why ask?" Walapai Charley sat outside the saloon with his back to the thin clapboard wall. He whittled on a small length of pine using the two-inch blade, all that remained of his brush with the sniping Private McCue.

Slocum slumped. He dropped to the boardwalk and scooted over, sitting beside the Walapai scout. Hoping Eastman's hearing would turn out differently, Slocum found no reason to stay in Prescott.

His mind drifted for a moment back to the all too brief meal with Moira Kelson. She had presented such a pretty picture— and she had offered him a percentage of the Three Card Monte, if he found a buyer for the worthless hole in the ground. Slocum had been around miners long enough to know someone would buy the shaft, no matter its condition. Stories of companies buying worthless pits only to find fabulous riches after a little more work were as beguiling as prospecting for the mineral in the first place. Nobody forgot how Jay

Gould had saved his fortune buying a played-out silver mine that eventually produced twenty million dollars in bullion.

He could sell the mine eventually, if he stayed in Prescott. That Moira would remain here until she received money from her brother's claim gave him a powerful incentive, also. But Slocum knew he could never return to Camp Beale Springs as a scout or in any other capacity. Captain Byrne had been acquitted of all wrongdoing in McCue's murder.

Worse, Henry Eastman had gone along with allowing the Walapai to strip their dead enemy and loot indiscriminately. Sherum's war party was one thing; allowing Chief Levy-Levy's men to do the same, especially with Byrne's approval, was not to be tolerated. Such a decision would only heighten tension between the troopers and their commander. What it would do to the growing animosity between the Walapai trying to settle peaceably around Beale Springs and the citizens of Prescott and Hardyville was something Slocum didn't want to be around to see.

He knew a tinderbox when he saw one. Before the month was out, the soldiers, civilians, and Levy-Levy's warriors would be shooting each other. And Sherum would sit back in his Black Mountains retreat and laugh—and continue to kill and plunder at will.

The future of Arizona Territory looked to be a bloody one, and all because Thomas Byrne drunkenly had murdered a handful of deserters from his own command.

"A month back I had considered riding to the coast, then going up to Oregon. They raise some fine horses there," Slocum said. He glanced over at Charley, working diligently on the hunk of pinewood. Shavings grew in a small pile between the Indian's legs, but Slocum could not figure out what it was Charley carved, if anything at all.

"You are a mean bronco buster. We could split the horses after gentling them and—"

"You want *me* to go with you to Oregon?" Charley showed surprise. He covered quickly and kept whittling. "Don't know this Oregon country. Heard it is wet. I like it dry. I like knowing where the watering holes are."

"Hunting there is good," Slocum said. "You don't have to spend days tracking down a single starving deer."

"Where's the challenge in that?"

Slocum had to laugh, though he knew Charley was never going to join him. He liked the scout and the way he had with animals. Two of them working a herd of Appaloosas could more than double the profit Slocum might enjoy. Still, it was asking a lot from a man who had never left Arizona Territory in all his born days to move to unknown country. Not everyone was as filled with wanderlust as John Slocum.

"There's nothing keeping me here," Slocum said. "It's been good riding with you, Charley." Slocum started to rise. Charley tossed his small knife and sank it into the boardwalk in front of Slocum.

"That silver mine," Charley said obliquely. "You could get a better price for it, and quicker, too, if Sherum was all settled peacefully next to Levy-Levy on the reservation."

"True," Slocum said, not knowing where this led.

"And the woman. The one with liquid gold for hair. Not as much meat on her bones as I like, but you're different. You have a real hankering for her."

Slocum did not respond to that. Riding off and leaving Moira would cause a hole in his life. For a spell.

"Byrne might be transferred if Sherum signs a treaty and keeps it," Charley went on. "Looks as if my brother's the axle and everything else turns around him."

"What are you saying?"

"If we talk to Sherum and get him to settle down with Levy-Levy's people, things get better for everyone."

"If the sky opened up and rained twenty-dollar gold pieces,

it'd be a good thing, too," Slocum said. "Not likely to happen."

"We can't do much about the rain. We can find Sherum. You and me. We find him, I talk to him."

"You are a talker," Slocum said. Charley smiled at this. "What's in it for you?"

"Byrne looks good, he gets promoted and sent somewhere else. The Walapai benefit from that, if a new commander is better. Might even take Gorman with him when he goes."

"That's a lot of 'might evens,' " Slocum said.

"You might even get to see the pretty lady again," Charley finished. He reached for the knife and pulled it from the board. He indicated Moira Kelson crossing the street and heading for her hotel. She didn't see Slocum.

"You might even be right," Slocum said.

Walapai Charley looked at him and waited.

"Where do you think we can find your half brother?" Slocum asked.

"Not Sherum's doing," Walapai Charley said as he studied the ground. The stagecoach heading for Fort Mojave had been ambushed and all passengers killed. The driver had been plugged but managed to survive a three-day trek through the desert before dying. Of the shotgun messenger there was no trace.

"The driver didn't say much more than he'd been attacked."

"White men did this. Boots. See?"

Slocum got down on his hands and knees and let the slanting afternoon light cast shadows in the shallow depression.

"Boots," he agreed. "Since we didn't find any trace of the guard, you think he might have joined in the robbery?"

Charley shrugged. "Doesn't matter. This isn't Sherum."

"That leaves the report of him in the foothills," Slocum

said, brushing off the dirt from his hands. This stagecoach holdup had been bloody, but Sherum hadn't committed the crime. Too many small details pointed to the shotgun messenger being in cahoots with the robbers. The tracks left by men wearing boots finished the incomplete picture. The Walapai wore moccasins. Sherum would never outfit his braves in boots to muddy the trail.

He was too good at doing that using other methods.

"Might be him. He moved his camp pretty quick after you came back with the red-haired woman," Charley said.

"Moira. Moira Kelson."

"The red-haired woman might have spooked Sherum," Charley went on, as if he had not heard Slocum. "Her hair is strange. He might see this as an omen."

"He moved his camp, but where?"

"There," Charley said with some finality. He turned and stared into the foothills of the Black Mountains. "Our ancestral home. He would return to land he knows best. From there he can strike without fear, knowing he has a secure camp awaiting him."

"Let's find some spoor," Slocum said, swinging into the saddle. The bay gelding he now rode protested the weight. They had ridden far these past five days, seldom resting. Slocum knew any horse race would go against them. Their mounts were exhausted and they were in little better condition. In spite of this, an energy filled him.

He felt *close* to Sherum. If only Charley's persuasive powers carried the day when they did find Sherum. Otherwise, they might fall into one of his traps and never be seen again.

Riding slowly, Slocum searched from one side of the road to the other. He missed a few details but nothing important. And because of his attention, he spotted Sherum's trail before Charley.

"There," he said suddenly. "Look at the trace running between those boulders. Heads into the foothills, about where you said Sherum might camp.''

"Horse dung," Charley said, his nose wrinkled. "Fresh. A day at the most. Who else might travel these hills?"

"Nobody," Slocum said. "There's more evidence." He pointed at patches of grass cropped close by grazing horses. More than one animal had been hobbled in a small glade beyond the boulders to clip the grass so thoroughly. He rode around the small glade, coming close to a line of trees running higher into the hills. Here he found a game path, but no deer had left the huge prints.

"He's getting careless," Slocum said. "Or he's luring us into a trap."

"He feels secure here. This is home," Charley said, but the Walapai scout did not immediately follow the trail. He dismounted and examined shrubs and the ground and even the distant mountains poking up above the treetops before deciding.

"He is secure here. There will not be a trap like before, but we will find sentries along this path. Miles from here will be where we find Sherum. Do we walk or do we ride a ways more?" Walapai Charley spoke to himself, debating the finer points of each plan.

Slocum came to a quicker conclusion. He drew the Winchester from its scabbard, tucked a spare box of ammo into his pocket and then hobbled the bay so it wouldn't wander off. The track disappeared through an increasingly dense forested area. A trap might be sprung at any turn along it, causing Slocum to consider walking parallel.

"You not riding, Slocum?"

He shook his head. He knew they might be long miles from Sherum's camp, yet he felt easier on foot where he could dodge and duck and find cover in a hurry, if necessary. Slocum had had his fill of getting horses shot out from under him. The paint had pulled up lame before he returned to Camp Beale Springs from Prescott. He wanted the bay rested and ready to gallop if the need arose and they had to withdraw in a hurry.

"Might be a good idea," Walapai Charley said, slipping from his horse. He checked his rifle, then started off at a ground-devouring pace. Slocum followed, not caring if he kept up with the Indian. He had to advance at his own pace to assure himself he wasn't going to be captured again.

Sherum would not have forgotten him from their first meeting. Slocum had humiliated Sherum so much the Walapai chief would never forget. Ever.

An hour into the forest brought them to a rising section of the path. Something about the lay of the land put Slocum on his guard. He saw Charley's shadow, drifting like smoke through the forest, stop and then simply vanish.

He went to ground, too. Seconds later he heard the clop-clop of horses approaching. Three braves rode past, not ten feet away. Slocum's finger rubbed back and forth on the rifle trigger, but he knew better than to shoot. Three warriors going on a scout meant Sherum's main camp lay just over the rise ahead.

Working on his belly, he came up beside Charley. The Indian sat with his back to a tree, eyes fixed on the notch in the forest through which the riders had come.

"There," he said. "Sherum camps there."

"What now?"

"We see if he is at home." Without another word, Charley wiggled through the forest quieter than any snake. Slocum followed, trying to imitate his friend's movement. In comparison he was clumsy, but he was still good enough to come up on two sentries without them knowing it.

Charley had disappeared, leaving Slocum to deal with the guards. He studied the matter a moment, waited to be sure the pair stood their watch out of sight of other guards, then he moved. Rising up behind one Walapai, he swung the rifle butt hard into the back of the man's head. The Walapai's head snapped forward, and he fell facedown onto the ground. He had not let out even a small moan. The suddenness of the attack froze the other where he stood. His eyes went wide as he stared at his fallen comrade.

Slocum took three quick steps and swung his rifle like a baseball bat. The barrel clipped the sentry on the temple. He stumbled back a step, then fell heavily. In a sitting position, he reached up to touch the spot at his temple now sluggishly bleeding. Slocum caught the other side of the Walapai's head with a return swing.

Both guards had fallen without uttering a sound. Dropping to his knees, Slocum checked first one and then the other for signs of life. He had only knocked them out. He let out a small sigh. His instincts told him to slit their throats, but he knew this would end Charley's chance for a palaver.

Working quickly, Slocum cut strips of buckskin from the two guards' leggings and secured them to a tree. More time was spent gagging them so they could do nothing but mutter. He tossed their weapons into a low ravine, then worked his way down the hillside in the direction of Sherum's camp. Cooking odors made his nose wrinkle and mouth water. Venison. The renegade ate well tonight. All Slocum had eaten in the past two days was jerky and trail biscuits washed down with tepid water.

One juniper at the side of the encampment dominated the area. Slocum climbed onto a limb ten feet above the ground, then lay flat, his rifle sticking out. He commanded most of the camp from his vantage.

He hoped he didn't have to make a quick retreat. From here he could fight well but would fall easy prey to anyone coming up on him from the forest.

Sighting along his rifle barrel, he centered on first one and then another of the warriors sitting around the fires, laughing and eating. Women worked to one side of the camp, mending torn garments and reprimanding playing children. If Slocum hadn't known better, he would have thought this was the camp of a peaceful tribe enjoying an evening of solitude.

Some spontaneous singing erupted, dying down as others joined in a joke. The abrupt silence that fell on the camp alerted Slocum to the single figure walking down the path and heading straight for the largest fire where Sherum ate his cooked venison dinner.

Slocum's finger tightened on the trigger when he saw a few braves lift their rifles and bows and arrows, intent on shooting Walapai Charley. Something in the scout's attitude caused them to draw back and let him pass.

Charley walked directly to his half brother and stood for a moment until Sherum nodded brusquely. Then Charley sank to his haunches and began talking.

Slocum didn't understand much of the Walapai tongue, but he knew Charley was giving his outlaw half brother a full recitation of the trouble he faced if he didn't come to Beale Springs and negotiate. Several times the name Levy-Levy was shouted, but always the two settled down to a quieter discussion.

But Slocum jerked and tightened his grip on the rifle when Sherum blasted to his feet and whipped out his knife. He slashed the air in front of Charley's face. Charley never flinched as Sherum continued to menace him.

The range was less than a hundred years, and Slocum had made harder shots many times. He needed only squeeze off the round that would end Sherum's life. But something stayed his shot. Sherum could have killed Charley with a single thrust and had not. What went on Slocum wasn't sure about, but he doubted Charley was going to be taken prisoner and tortured.

After a few more seconds of posturing and mock battle,

Sherum settled down again. He drove the knife into the ground between them. Charley reached down, pulled the knife from the dirt and handed it back to his half brother.

Then Charley stood, turned, and walked from the camp, never looking back. Slocum guessed that Charley had been successful. Now all he had to do was get out of the Walapai camp without being seen and celebrate the victory with the scout.

On cat's feet, John Slocum dropped from the limb and faded into darkness, leaving behind the Walapai encampment and their chief to join Charley where they had left their horses.

"So?" he asked when he finally spotted Charley. The scout looked glum. "What'd you say?"

"Everything I could think of that would persuade him," Charley said. "It worked. Sherum will parley."

"Why so gloomy?" Slocum had to ask. "You succeeded where half the cavalry in Arizona has failed. You stopped the pillaging and brought peace to an entire territory."

"Perhaps so," Charley said, "but what have I done to Sherum? A treaty sealed in liquor is no treaty at all. Have I done a terrible thing to my brother by luring him to Beale Springs for treaty talks?"

Slocum didn't have an answer for that. The image of Captain Byrne wobbling as he signed the treaty was all too clear.

15

"Nobody seems too excited over the new treaty," Slocum observed. He swatted his bay on the rump and got the horse into the corral with the troopers' mounts.

"Might not believe it," said Walapai Charley. "After so much killing, quiet can deafen a man."

"Nobody's treating us like we did much, either," Slocum said. "I didn't expect a medal, but we *did* get Sherum in to parley. And he *did* sign the treaty. His name's right there alongside Levy-Levy's. I doubt Sherum has more than a dozen renegade braves loose in the Black Mountains any more. Less," Slocum said with some satisfaction. A few braves refused to follow Sherum to the tranquility of the reservation, calling him a traitor just as Sherum had called Levy-Levy one months earlier. But the negotiations had gone well.

"Dan Smith did a good job translating. Maybe that's why no one's so excited about Sherum settling down. They don't know how Smith changed what was said into nice, easy-toswallow words." Charley laughed at this and shook his head. Of the two dozen people at the peace conference, only he and a few others understood the bitter insults initially uttered and the way Smith had turned them and translated them into lesser slanders for the sake of harmony.

Slocum jumped onto the top rail of the corral and began building himself a cigarette. He needed the soft smoke in his lungs to calm him after working like a dog all day long. Garrison duty wore on him, as it did on most of the soldiers. Still, it was a comforting thought to know he was likely to still have his scalp at sunrise. Sherum had led them a merry chase and had killed more than his share, but that was all past.

Sherum had agreed to meet with Captain Byrne and Chief Levy-Levy to discuss peace. Byrne had done little enough of the talking, leaving most of it to Henry Eastman. Slocum knew a bit of the details and cared nothing for anything except the quiet that had fallen on the area since the official signing a few days back.

The Walapai reservation stretched to the north of Beale Springs and gave them plenty of hunting ground. With the additional food given by the camp—especially now that John McCue was no longer stealing it—the Indians need not stay on the warpath. They would be fed and could live in peace with their brothers and the white man.

Slocum sucked in smoke, held it for a moment, then let it out to curl around his face. The still, hot summer day held the smoke in front of him. He blew a second time and caused it to curl away. That was the way he felt about Sherum agreeing to parley. It was tangible, and yet it disappeared without a trace at the most invisible of touches. Who remembered the troubles now that everything was quiet when the Walapai filed into the camp for their weekly rations?

"Too bad Captain Byrne doesn't have more of a hand in it," Slocum said. "I don't cotton much to the man and his heavy drinking, but deep down, in spite of being a back-shooting son of a bitch, he has treated the Walapai decently.''

Charley laughed and climbed onto the rough fence beside Slocum. He pulled his own fixings out from a shirt pocket and expertly rolled a cigarette. A quick trip of tongue over the rolling paper and he had his own ready to go. Slocum silently lit Charley's from the glowing tip of his smoke.

''I'll never understand you. Byrne kills the deserters and lets the scouts strip them for booty, but you think he is the one who ought to have negotiated. Eastman turned out to be a straight shooter.''

''You'd rather have Henry Eastman doing the chore?'' This amazed Slocum. ''His tongue flaps at both ends when he talks.''

''He speaks for those in Washington.''

Slocum looked at Charley for a moment, hunting for any trace of sarcasm. He thought the Walapai joshed him, but he could not be sure.

''Byrne knows the situation with the rations, how the hunting grounds ought to be divvied up, everything. Eastman obviously is looking to his own behind.''

''He has much to cover, then,'' Charley said. The scout jumped lightly to the ground and walked away. Again Slocum could not tell if Charley was putting him on.

After walking around the camp for a half hour and finding nothing to hold his interest, Slocum turned toward the enlisted men's barracks. A few penny-ante games of poker looked promising until he saw how little money actually exchanged hands. The soldiers played not to get rich but to break the boredom. If anyone walked away with too big a pot, it would start a fight.

Which would be as good as letting the players take turns winning. It interrupted the crushing burden of monotonous garrison duty.

"You on patrol tonight, Slocum?" asked Corporal Framingham.

"Not until next week. I reckoned the captain would have cut me loose by this time. Sherum signing the treaty put an end to my usefulness."

Framingham laughed at this. "To hear Lieutenant Gorman tell it, none of us is worth a bucket of spit, much less our salaries."

Slocum said nothing. Gorman and his big yellow dog were constant reminders of earlier days at the camp—days filled with corruption and outright hatred. He avoided the lieutenant whenever possible, and that pleased everyone. Slocum had never found the proof that McCue worked at Gorman's behest when it came to selling the surplus supplies or that he had been with McCue during the dry-gulching, but admitting the lieutenant's only concern might be stark hatred of the Walapai because of what happened to his family stuck in his craw. Slocum wanted charges filed to get rid of Gorman once and for all time.

"Reckon I will be moving on soon enough," Slocum said. "I considered it a month or two back after Levy-Levy signed the treaty. It's even quieter now with Sherum settling in."

"I got to report to the sergeant of the guard. I pulled sentry duty again," said Framingham. "If you're going into Prescott, pick me up some tobacco, will you, Slocum?" The corporal fished in his pocket and came out with a dime. Slocum caught it easily as it spun in the air.

"Why not get it through the sutler?"

Framingham shrugged. "Hasn't had so much as a sprig for a week or more. Something wrong getting supplies in, maybe."

Slocum frowned. This was the first he had heard of supply trouble, but he had been keeping to himself a great deal. When he ate, it was as likely to be with Walapai Charley and his family as it was in the mess hall.

"Captain Byrne's not having any trouble getting his liquor," Slocum said. He heard the commander singing loudly and in his off-key baritone. On the step in front of Byrne's office stood Henry Eastman and Samuel Gorman. The lieutenant held out a sheet of paper. Eastman took it and stuffed it away hurriedly, as if afraid someone might see it.

Slocum reckoned it might be a requisition for more whiskey. Byrne went through a prodigious supply every week.

Hitching up his gun belt, Slocum headed for the corral and saddled his horse. Camp Beale Springs was wearing him down like water dripping slowly on a stone. No single drop amounted to much, but the everyday tedium tore away at his gut. It was time to move on, after he finished his business in Prescott.

The ride into town went quickly for him. It felt good letting the wind wash past his leathery face again. It made him think he was actually footloose and fancy free once more instead of tied down as a cavalry scout with no enemy to find or territory to map.

He reached Prescott in jig time and dismounted, wondering where he might find Moira. Rather than hunt for her, he went to the land office and ducked his head inside.

"Joe?" he called, not seeing anyone in the office.

"That you, Slocum? I wondered when you'd get back to me." The land agent came in from the side yard, lugging a heavy ledger of recorded deeds. Joe Sanderson dropped it onto his desk. The wooden legs quivered under the weight and threatened to give out, but once more they held.

"Any takers on the Three Card Monte?"

"Got a mining company looking to expand into the area," Joe said. The dark-haired young clerk settled in a chair and hiked his feet to his desk. After lacing his fingers behind his head, he said, "I can sweet-talk them into sending a representative out from San Francisco, but it might take a week or so.''

"I'm not going anywhere," Slocum said. "Think we can get a good price out of them?"

"I'm banking on it," Joe said. "With the Monte and five other mines along that same canyon all rolled into a neat package, I can get more than I ever could selling them separately. Truth is, Slocum, the assays on the Monte aren't very promising."

"I appreciate it, Joe."

"Yeah, right," the land agent said. He dropped his feet to the floor and wrestled open the ledger to begin work. "And don't forget that ten percent 'appreciation fee' when I pass over the deed."

Slocum left, feeling good about selling Moira's legacy so quickly. Chief Sherum being on the warpath had dropped interest in buying mining property, but now that peace settled like a comfortable cotton blanket over the territory, all was well. Mining companies would drift back unless a big strike brought them flocking like vultures to a juicy bit of carrion.

"John. John!" Moira Kelson waved from across the street. Slocum couldn't keep a big smile from crossing his face. He thought she was about the most beautiful woman he had ever seen the first time he had laid eyes on her. Every time after put that to the lie. She grew increasingly lovely until it made his heart ache knowing she would soon enough be going her own way.

After the Three Card Monte sold and she had her money, there was nothing to keep her in Prescott—or even in Arizona Territory. For all that, Slocum knew there was nothing holding him here. It was only a matter of time before he got his share of the sale and moved on, to Oregon or Idaho or Texas or somewhere that wasn't hot, arid Arizona.

He dodged the wagons and horses making their way down

the middle of Prescott's busy street and joined Moira. The sun caught her red hair and turned it into spun gold. He would miss seeing her like this.

He would miss her. Period.

"What's the news about the mine?" she asked, enthusiasm bubbling.

"Good. The agent's sent out a call on the telegraph to a dozen different mining companies. One's bound to send a surveyor out to look over the property. In a way, we were lucky. With Sherum killing miners, all the claims in that valley are up for sale or simply abandoned."

"It is a pity Monty and Sean worked a worthless mine," she said, sighing heavily. "I only wish the matter were over."

"In a hurry to leave Prescott?" Slocum asked.

"It's not that, John," she said. "The troubles are beginning all over again, and I want to be free of the mine before anything happens. We ought to be far away when new conflict begins."

"What are you talking about? Levy-Levy and Sherum are both settled on their reservation land. They have plenty to eat, and there's no reason for them to—" He bit off the words when he saw the surprise on Moira's face.

"It's not that way, John," she said, studying his face for any sign he was joking. "The word is all over town how Eastman is moving Sherum and the others farther and farther away from Beale Springs."

"I never heard where the reservation ended," Slocum said, "but that doesn't mean Eastman is out to swindle the Walapai."

"He doesn't call it that, but what name would you put to hiding all the Walapai on a far-off reservation near Fort Mojave?"

"Fort Mojave? With the Mojave Indians?" Slocum didn't know whether to laugh or get angry at such a notion. "The

Mojave Indians are farmers. They live along the Colorado River. The Walapai are hunters. There'd be nothing for them to hunt along the river.''

When Moira said nothing, Slocum got a cold lump in the pit of his stomach.

"Who's been telling you this?"

"Everyone knows it," Moira said. "Come inside, John. I thought you knew all this." She took his arm and steered him into the hotel lobby. She sat in a chair next to a couch where Slocum settled in. Taking his hand in hers, she held it tightly. "We must sell the mine quickly to be out of the territory before everyone is massacred."

"*That's* the rumor?"

"No one here considers it such," Moira said. "Eastman is stealing food, as McCue did. He sells it to the less scrupulous merchants in town. They have to paint out the cavalry insignia on many of the crates before displaying it in their stores."

"Gorman," Slocum muttered. He had seen Gorman hand Eastman a paper back at the camp. Was the lieutenant the mastermind behind new theft of military supplies?

"The land intended for the Walapai is to be sold. There is some official paper being prepared that will make this possible."

"The Walapai will never leave prime hunting land. Levy-Levy would never agree. Sherum would die before he stuck a seed in the ground to farm." Even as the words came from his lips, Slocum understood the powder keg under them. Both Walapai chiefs had signed the peace treaty—but the treaty promised hunting land. He and Walapai Charley had brought Sherum in and convinced him to settle down.

If Sherum went back on the warpath, he was likely to take Chief Levy-Levy and all his braves along. Blood would flow from Flagstaff to Bisbee and make the San Carlos Apache problems look like a Sunday school passion play.

"This can't be right. Eastman wouldn't renege on the deal he made with the Walapai. If he tried, Byrne would stop him from doing anything. Byrne favors the Walapai."

"Unless Captain Byrne was too far in his cups."

"Gorman," Slocum said again. If the lieutenant kept his commander liquored up and drunker than a lord, this gave him a free hand to do as he pleased at the camp and with the reservation land promised to the Walapai. Gorman and Eastman made a powerful team, seemingly working with the full knowledge and blessing of those back in Washington.

"We must hurry to sell the mine, John. There is so little time. I feel as if the walls were crushing in on me."

"Get on the first stagecoach out of here. Head west, go to California. I can catch up with you there after the Three Card Monte is sold—if you trust me with the money."

"Oh, John, don't be silly. Of course I trust you." He heard the ring of sincerity in her voice.

"I want to ride back to Beale Springs and get to the bottom of this. When you find out where the first stage will take you, leave a note with Joe Sanderson at the land office."

"John, I don't want to leave you behind."

"The whole territory will go up in smoke, if what you say is true. I don't want to be worrying about you if trouble does erupt."

Leaving Moira Kelson as he rode back to Camp Beale Springs was about the hardest thing Slocum had ever done.

16

Before he rode within hailing distance, Slocum saw the difference at Camp Beale Springs. When he left hours earlier, Slocum had watched the sentry struggle to keep from nodding off. Now the entire post swarmed like an anthill with boiling water poured down it. Two companies toiled on the parade grounds, cleaning rifles and sharpening bayonets. Another company worked diligently waxing their saddles. And in the midst of the turmoil strode Captain Thomas Byrne, once more the epitome of the U.S. Cavalry commander.

"Captain," called Slocum, hitting the ground and pulling his horse to a halt. "Heard rumors in town that—"

"The rumors are true, Slocum. Sherum and half the Walapai warriors have left their land and gone back on the warpath. This might be the shortest treaty in the history of the United States of America."

Slocum looked past Byrne to where Henry Eastman and Lieutenant Gorman stood. The two argued again, and as before, Slocum saw papers changing hands as if the pair did not want anyone else to see. Samuel Gorman drew an envelope from his jacket and stepped closer to the Indian agent. Eastman grabbed the envelope and hurriedly tucked it into his own coat pocket.

"We move out within the hour, Slocum. Be ready. I will not let this search for Sherum and his renegades linger as I did before. We catch him quickly and bring him to justice!" Striking a pose, Byrne made a noble figure. Slocum wondered if the captain expected a picture to be taken. As the thought passed through his head, Slocum was jolted by the thunder of the camp cannon firing.

"We must be ready to repel attack as well as launch it," Byrne said. He marched off, yelling orders and gathering his junior officers behind him. Gorman said something more to the nervous Eastman, then joined the others with his commander.

Slocum went to get rations and additional ammunition from the armorer. He found Walapai Charley sitting on a rain barrel, carefully whittling at a piece of fresh pinewood. The short two-inch-long knife worked intricate patterns in the soft wood. From the pile of chips at the scout's feet, he had been working for quite a while.

"Just got back from town," Slocum said. "Reckon you were right. Now's not the time to move on. What happened to make Sherum bolt so quick from the reservation?"

Charley's lips curled in a mocking smile.

"You ought to be a medicine man. You're better than any of those quacks in the Walapai tribe," Charley said. "Seeing the future is a rare gift given by the gods."

"The land," Slocum said, ignoring the scout's change of direction. "Eastman has done something to keep the Walapai off it."

"The reservation is along the Colorado River. 'Farm it,' he

said to hunters. We are not Mojaves who can poke the ground with a stick and watch corn sprout. We need to find deer. We need to hunt.''

Slocum noted how Charley now included himself with Sherum every time he spoke of the tribe. ''We need to hunt,'' Charley had said. Not ''they need to hunt.''

''I heard rumors in town about Eastman shortchanging the rations, as McCue had done. Any truth to that?''

''Who can say? Sherum wasn't supposed to get any food for another month.''

''No rations from the camp and no land to hunt on. Little wonder he took off running.'' Slocum marveled at the stupidity of the men entrusted with administering the peace. Byrne was a bad choice; he stayed drunk too much of the time to notice anything wrong. In the field, he was a decent commander, but others ought to run his garrison. Slocum had seen this defect in commanders before—and had learned the troubles it caused.

''More left with him than surrendered days ago. Too many with Levy-Levy had grown unhappy. Can you blame them?''

Slocum said nothing. He and Charley had risked their lives to get Sherum in to the peace conference. Others such as Daniel Smith had given their time and best effort to convincing the rampaging Walapai chief of the government's good intentions. In a few short days, Eastman had ruined everything.

Henry Eastman and Lieutenant Samuel Gorman, if Slocum was any judge.

''Are you still scouting for the captain?'' Slocum asked.

All he got in reply was a curt nod. Seeing Charley wasn't inclined to say much more, Slocum went to get what supplies he could. The troopers always managed to get the bulk of the supplies, leaving the scouts to fend for themselves. No matter that the scouts were always on the knife-edge of danger and miles away from reinforcement, usually needing to ride fast and with little time for hunting.

As he readied his gear, Slocum wondered why he bothered. Byrne might bring back Sherum and the renegade warriors to a reservation along the Colorado River, but they would return to the same troubles. And that only spelled a worse uprising down the road. He rode out onto the parade ground, intending to tell Byrne he was quitting. Let the dust settle around Beale Springs, get Sherum situated properly with the other Walapai, and then Slocum knew he could sell the Three Card Monte fast.

And what then? He wasn't sure, but it had to be a better future than endlessly chasing the wiliest warrior he had ever fought.

Slocum wheeled his bay around, hunting for Walapai Charley. The Indian scout was nowhere to be seen, and Captain Byrne had already formed his columns.

"You ready, Slocum? Head on east and—"

"Where's Charley?" Slocum interrupted. "I didn't figure he would take this long to get ready for the expedition."

"He's not accompanying us. He has chosen to remain with Levy-Levy rather than face that blackguard Sherum." Byrne pulled himself straighter in the saddle and fixed his bloodshot eyes on Slocum. "You are not intending to similarly desert us, are you, Slocum?"

Slocum had been, but he understood Charley's motives for not going with the column more than he did his own for not quitting. Charley had persuaded Sherum to come to the peace talks, and Eastman had made the scout out to be a liar and a fool. All that Charley promised had turned to dust in days after Chief Sherum had surrendered.

To go after Sherum again seemed the height of hypocrisy. Slocum was sure that was the way Charley felt, too.

"East, you say?"

Byrne nodded briskly, then turned to pass his commands

along to Gorman and the other lieutenants at the heads of their companies. Slocum trotted from Camp Beale Springs and turned toward the east. It was going to be a long scout, and he had to do it alone.

A blind man couldn't miss the trail. Slocum had followed Sherum and his braves on a roundabout course over the last week, and they had circled and dodged—and led him directly to this canyon in the Black Mountains. The terrain was gorgeous in a stark way. Less desert growth here signaled higher elevation, and there wasn't much in the way of spruce and fir at this level. The scrubby trees were oaks, cottonwoods, juniper, and even a few stunted mesquites. The palo verde and acacia found in hotter areas had vanished.

With that disappearance came an uneasiness Slocum could not put to rest. He had followed Sherum enough to know the Walapai chief did nothing without a reason. The obvious trail leading into the canyon was a trap.

"You have nothing to prove that, Slocum," complained Lieutenant Gorman. "A feeling, that's all. I say Sherum got careless. We have to ride after him and drag him out, dead or alive. We *have* to or no Indian in this territory will ever respect us."

"It's a trap," Slocum said tiredly. He turned to Captain Byrne, but the officer wasn't listening. He had finished off an entire saddlebag of liquor on their hunt, emptying a bottle just a few minutes prior to Slocum's warning. Byrne was in no condition to make a command decision. Leaving it to the hotheaded Gorman would get most of the command killed.

"He can't know, Captain," Gorman said angrily. "Slocum's not been into the canyon. Sherum left a trail. We have him!"

"Bull on in and he'll have you—and your head on a war lance," Slocum shot back. He wished Walapai Charley had come with them. He could use the scout's quiet conviction and obvious expertise to reverse the decision to lose hundreds of men needlessly in an ambush.

"What is our mission, Mr. Slocum?" asked Byrne.

"Get Sherum back to the reservation," Slocum said. "The one you promised, not the patch of land along the Colorado River."

"That is a political matter beyond my control," Byrne said with drunken solemnity. "I did not negotiate the contract. Treaty. Whatever it was. Henry Eastman did."

Slocum watched Samuel Gorman carefully. A small smile tugged at the corners of the lieutenant's lips. Eastman and Gorman were in cahoots, divvying up land and property belonging to the Walapai tribe. Byrne was a dupe and unable to stop the theft. Who could? Slocum didn't know, but it wasn't going to be him if he followed Byrne into this obvious trap.

"I'll go ahead at twilight," Slocum suggested. "It may take most of the night to find how Sherum has his braves arrayed against you, but I am sure he does. There might be some way you can attack if I find weaknesses in his ambush plan."

"Let Sherum get away? Are you suggesting we give that bloody-handed guerrilla even one minute longer than he has now? He will escape!" cried Gorman. "Are you in league with him, Slocum?"

"For two bits, I'd let you lead the charge into that canyon," Slocum said. "The only trouble is that I'd never collect, unless I took the money off your corpse."

Gorman turned red in the face and reached for his saber. Slocum hoped he would whip out the long blade. It would give him adequate reason to put a slug in the lieutenant's worthless body.

"Gentlemen, we advance slowly, wary of any possible trap Sherum might have set for us," Byrne said.

"The ambush is there. You've felt the teeth of his traps

before,'' Slocum reminded the captain.

"All the more reason to advance. We can hunt endlessly for him. This way we can find him.''

"A good way of finding you have your head cut off,'' Slocum grumbled. In spite of his misgivings, Slocum rode off to one side of the column as Byrne led his troopers into the canyon. The fading light sent long shadows dancing onto the canyon floor and obscured huge areas from sight. Slocum wished Byrne would delay entry into the canyon until after the sun set, if he had to blunder ahead at all without reconnoitering. As it was, the soldiers would be illuminated and Sherum's warriors hidden in shadows on either side of the canyon.

Two hundred men entered the mouth of the canyon. Slocum held his breath. Nothing happened. He trotted in front of the column, keen eyes scanning the ground. Signs showed at least twenty of Sherum's braves had passed this way recently, possibly within hours. The more uneasy Slocum grew, the more Gorman insisted they pick up the pace.

"There are no Indians awaiting us,'' Gorman said. "They are cowards. They are craven dogs, whipped and running with their tails between their legs. They fear the might of the U.S. Cavalry!''

Slocum didn't bother answering such a ridiculous claim. Sherum had never shown a moment's fear fighting the soldiers and wasn't about to now. The Walapai chief fought to regain his land. He would never leave the territory he called his home.

A mile into the canyon and Slocum saw no hint of the ambush he feared. Two miles. He began to think he had been wrong. The spoor increased, discarded eagle feathers, beads, and even broken arrows and lances littering the path now. The Walapai had galloped along this narrow dirt path in a powerful hurry. The items left behind might not be serviceable but they could be fixed with a little work and turned back into useful items.

It was almost as if Sherum left his detritus as a lure. A careful man on a riverbank dangling his pole into the water, hook carrying just the right bait for his elusive finned quarry.

"Captain Byrne," Slocum said, riding back to the officer, "camp here for the night. Get a defensive perimeter set up. Don't ride on in the dark. You'll only fall headlong into trouble."

"We have to overtake them, Slocum," Byrne pointed out. His breath was strong enough to knock over a mule, and he wobbled in the saddle. Slocum had never seen the man hitting the bottle as he rode, but the effects were unmistakable. The bluecoats' commander was completely unfit to make any decision of importance quickly.

Worse, Slocum would have to appeal to Lieutenant Gorman, as senior officer, to override the captain's orders. Considering Gorman's hatred of the Walapai and other Indian tribes, sanity was as likely as a snowstorm in hell.

"Let me double back and see if our trail is clear, if we have to retreat," Slocum said.

"Retreat? War is never won by retreat. Only by advance. I thought you knew better, Slocum." Thomas Byrne almost toppled from his saddle as he tried to rear back in mock anger at such effrontery.

The pounding of a horse's hooves sounded in the dim light. Slocum glanced past Byrne's shoulder, in the direction of the rear of the column. A messenger galloped hard on a lathered horse to bring the report.

"Captain, Captain Byrne!" the courier shouted. "We been shot at! They're comin' at us from all sides!"

"What are you saying? Who is being attacked?"

"Lieutenant Hurst, sir. His entire company is pinned down."

"I hear no gunfire," Byrne said. Hardly had the words left his lips than the echoes from a hundred rifles rumbled to put his statement to the lie.

Then Slocum saw dark forms rising from shadows as close as a few feet away. The Walapai had covered themselves with blankets in shallow trenches, piling brush over the blankets. Now was the time for them to spring the deadly trap.

Slocum whipped out his Colt Navy and fired point-blank into one Walapai brave intent on sending an arrow through Captain Byrne's chest. But the confusion spread rapidly as the troopers' mounts reared and they fought to control them. Order was lost in seconds as Sherum's fighters shot both arrows and bullets into the cavalry's ranks.

The trap had been sprung, and Slocum could do nothing about it.

17

Strong hands groped for Slocum. He kicked hard but found himself pulled out of the saddle from behind. He fell through the air, arms windmilling as he went. He crashed hard into a frantically grasping Walapai brave. The two of them went to the ground, Slocum coming out on top. Rolling fast, he swung himself about and got his feet under him. As the Walapai tried to regain his own stance, Slocum launched himself like a Fourth of July rocket.

Shoulder crushing into the man's belly, Slocum bowled the brave over. He kept driving his shoulder into the hard gut he found until he pinned the brave to the ground. A quick movement drew his knife and sent it into the brave's heart. Jerking like a fish out of water, the Walapai tried to convince his body he had not died. He failed.

Slocum had no time to catch his breath. All around him the battle raged. Fully one in ten of the troopers had perished in the first onslaught. The Walapai receded like the ocean's tide, only to return stronger than ever. They used bow and arrow and war lance rather than rifles, telling Slocum their ammunition was limited. This lack did little to prevent the carnage.

Through it all rode Captain Thomas Byrne. He shouted orders and fired his six-shooter and then drew his saber and launched a one-man charge through the middle of the battle. His blade sang a deadly song as he hacked left and right. Somehow, the sight of their commander so fearlessly attacking rallied the cavalry. The sergeants and corporals regained control of their squads, then the lieutenants found how best to send their companies against the Walapai.

As if grasping at ocean water, they found the Indians slipping away soundlessly into the gathering dusk.

"Bugler, sound assembly!" cried Byrne. He waved his bloody saber over his head, sending droplets into the night. Slocum admired the man in that moment—and then Byrne seemed to simply deflate. He slumped forward and clung to his saddle horn, slowly falling to one side.

Slocum caught the officer and lowered him to the ground.

"You wounded, Captain?" he asked. The reek of rotgut whiskey almost overwhelmed him when Byrne answered.

"I'm right as rain, Slocum. Just a spot of dizziness. Nothing for it but a good fight." Byrne struggled to his feet and weaved about, the sword dangling forgotten in his hand.

Somehow, Thomas Byrne had gone from hero to fool in the span of a heartbeat. Slocum began to doubt they would ever escape if the captain didn't shape up fast.

"Sir," reported Lieutenant Hurst, "half my troopers are dead or wounded. We cannot forge a decent attack. I recommend we retreat."

"Can't do that, Lieutenant," Slocum spoke up. He grabbed Byrne and held the officer erect. "Unless I miss my guess, Sherum's got the entire trail out of here lined with more of his braves. If they don't rush us in an all-out attack, they will cut us to ribbons one trooper at a time."

"We cannot stay here," protested the brash young lieutenant.

"We need leadership," cut in Samuel Gorman. "I'm senior officer. I'll assume command and—"

"There's nothing wrong with Captain Byrne," Slocum said, not wanting either Byrne or Gorman in charge. He had seen Joseph Hurst in action and liked the man's coolheadedness. Two of his noncoms were worthy of their rank, also. One of them, Sergeant Andrew Donnelly, limped up to report.

"Slocum's right. I saw them forming behind us. We need daylight to fight free. If we try retreating now, we'll be buzzard bait in the wink of an eye."

"What're you saying? We cannot be trapped. I won't permit it!" shouted Byrne. "We're after Sherum. He's not going to slip away again. We found him, we now take him into custody."

The men exchanged glances. Byrne hiccuped and sat heavily, resting his head against the hilt of his saber, now stuck point first into the dirt.

"He is in no condition to command. We will all die if he—"

Slocum cut Gorman off before he got up a full head of steam. "He's just led a successful skirmish. Maybe he's a mite tired." Slocum eyed Hurst and the sergeants to see how they responded. Hurst and Donnelly spoke quietly. The young second lieutenant wanted command badly, Slocum saw, but the older, more experienced Sergeant Donnelly argued against it.

"We'll patrol a defensive perimeter to keep them at bay until a better plan can be formulated," Hurst said. He glowered at Gorman, challenging the first lieutenant to contradict him. Gorman had enough sense to nod and then salute, as if dismissing Hurst.

"Drink," Byrne said. "I need a drink. Helluva fight makes

a man thirsty. Join me, Slocum?''

''Your bottle's broken,'' Slocum said, searching the officer's saddlebags. He found two untapped bottles. He heaved
them into the twilight. The crash of glass against rock and the
liquid gurgle afterward told of lost whiskey.

''Why'd you do that?''

''Sergeant Donnelly, can you see to getting a fire started, a
small one, and some hot coffee into Captain Byrne? He's
sorely in need of it.''

''Right away,'' Donnelly said.

''And then go see if Lieutenant Hurst needs you on the
picket line,'' Slocum said.

The sergeant obeyed Slocum without question. Gorman
swung about, furious at having his power usurped by a mere
scout. He shoved his chest hard against Slocum, trying to back
him down. Slocum refused to budge an inch. Eyes locked, they
engaged in a staring contest.

''I am in charge,'' Gorman said hotly. ''I am ranking officer
after Byrne. You will not issue orders, and I will see that any
of my men who obey you are court-martialed.''

''You want your scalp dangling from a Walapai war
lance?''

''You don't scare me, Slocum.'' His words were steely, but
Gorman backed off a little.

''It's not me you ought to be afraid of, Gorman. It's them.
Sherum's got more than the handful of warriors with him.
How many Walapai left their reservation?''

''We don't know,'' he said. Slocum saw that Gorman lied.
He said nothing, and the silence forced the rest of the infor-
mation from the lieutenant's lips.

''Levy-Levy left, too. About half his warriors rode with him
to join Sherum.''

''We're up against both Sherum *and* Levy-Levy?'' Slocum
spat in contempt for the military. He ought to have been told,

but would he have scouted for Byrne if he had? Slocum didn't
know.

"Get that filthy stuff away from me," came Byrne's petu-
lant words. He tried to force the battered cup holding tepid
coffee from Donnelly's hands. The sergeant motioned for Corporal Framingham to come and be sure their commander got
the coffee down. Donnelly left to rejoin Lieutenant Hurst at
the rear of the column.

"We need to know how many casualties we took in the
ambush," Slocum said. "From that you might be able to con-
coct a decent plan to save all our hides."

Gorman seemed to realize for the first time the seriousness
of their situation. He glared at Byrne, then did a parade ground
about-face and marched off, gathering his men about him as
he went. Slocum knew Chief Sherum—and Levy-Levy—
could have killed every last soldier in the trap if they had faded
away, regrouped, and then struck again. The confusion over
command in the cavalry's ranks would have guaranteed the
Walapais' success.

As it stood, Slocum wasn't sure if Sherum and Levy-Levy
weren't going to win simply through attrition, no matter how
much they argued between themselves. Standing back a few
yards and sending occasional arrows winging through the
horse soldiers as they cowered in fear might be enough to
insure their victory.

"Slocum, you shouldn't have broken my bottles. I need
whiskey." Byrne appeared a little more sober, but not much.

"Be an officer. Command your men and try not to lose too
many before I get back," Slocum said.

"Where are you going?"

"To find out what we're up against." Slocum reached down
and rubbed his fingers against the edge of a charred twig.
Smearing the soot on his cheeks, he set off into the night to
find the enemy.

He didn't have far to go.

•   •   •

Less than twenty yards away from where the troopers crouched behind rocks and trees, praying for dawn, Slocum found the first Walapai brave. The mound of earth in front of him moved slightly, and Slocum knew he had to be more careful. He had almost blundered onto the brave's hiding place under a thin blanket of tree limbs.

Sinking to the ground, Slocum advanced slowly until he was only feet away. He heard the shallow, rhythmic breathing of the hidden warrior. Rather than attack, Slocum moved away, seeking others ready to ambush the soldiers. A ten-minute foray convinced Slocum he was alone with this spy.

He returned silently, hand on his knife. Another few minutes put him into position for the kill. As he surged forward, intent on the hidden Indian, he knew he had made a mistake. Slocum crashed down onto an empty hidey-hole, his knife slicing through underbrush camouflaged with a saddle blanket.

Slocum cursed under his breath. He had made too much noise attacking a stalking-horse. He pushed clear of the covered brush and rolled fast to the side in time to avoid an arrow in the back. Slocum had fallen easily into a trap set by a master.

A second shaft sang through the air in Slocum's direction, but he was already in motion and scrambling for cover heavy enough to protect him from more arrows. He flopped on his belly, then dug his toes into the dry dirt, waiting for the proper moment to attack. Another arrow missed him by a handbreadth. Slocum launched himself straight for the shadowy warrior, knife preceding him. He slashed and drew a thin bloody line along a sinewy arm.

The Walapai grunted in pain and dropped the bow. But try as he might, Slocum couldn't close with him. The brave retreated into the night, swallowed by darkness. But Slocum felt his enemy's presence. The brave had not run far. He waited. He waited to kill.

Slocum knew he would never scout the true strength of the force holding Byrne's troopers captive with this single brave dogging his tracks. Moreover, the private battle took on a personal tone. Slocum had been snookered by the blanket and brush. He wasn't going to be as easily duped a second time.

To launch his attack straight ahead would have been foolish. But Slocum thought furiously. His opponent kept ahead of him, trying to anticipate his every move. To move forward without zigzagging or hunting for cover was suicidal. Better to take his time.

Slocum ran flat-out straight ahead, knife ready. He caught the brave by surprise. The Walapai had figured he would be more cautious, do the sensible thing. Slocum's arms circled the broad shoulders and carried the brave to the ground. Trying to get his knife into play proved more difficult than holding the brave to the ground.

Changing his tactics, Slocum tried to wrap his hands around the Walapai's throat. It was like trying to hold on to a wriggling mountain-stream trout. The brave slipped from Slocum's grip and got behind him. Slocum ducked his head down fast, crushing his chin down onto his chest as he waited for the thick arm to circle his throat.

It didn't come.

As Slocum had startled his adversary before with a frontal attack, so now did the Walapai dumbfound Slocum. The Indian simply disappeared.

Slocum dropped to hands and knees, listening hard for sounds of movement. He had only to return to Byrne's encampment and he would have relative safety for the night. But he had come out to scout, to find Sherum's strengths and weaknesses. One lone brave stood in the way, and Slocum took it as a personal challenge.

Small noises tempted Slocum to follow a game trail over a low rise. He resisted the urge. He realized he was playing a dangerous game of cat and mouse.

"He's thinking of this the same way I am," Slocum realized. In spite of the seriousness of the hunt, Slocum felt a rush of energy and knew he would not break off until one or the other lay dead. He felt as if a gunfighter had called him out. This was a challenge he could not deny.

Moving off the game trail, Slocum found a cottonwood tree and climbed to the lowest limb. Laying flat on it, he clutched his knife and waited. How long would it take for curiosity to bring his rival out?

Too long, Slocum decided. He licked his lips, then let out a low moan. A second moan sounded, louder and longer. Then he cut it off, knowing too much would alert his foe rather than draw him in for the easy kill.

Slocum blinked when he thought he saw shadows moving. Then his eyes fixed on a spot at the top of the ridge. The movement continued and came closer. He considered another low moan, then knew he had baited the hook enough. All he had to do was reel in his catch.

He gripped down tighter on his knife hilt, judged distances and times. Seconds. Closer. The Walapai was now outlined a few yards away. Slocum breathed in shallow gusts, not wanting to alert the brave with too much noise.

Closer. The Indian crept on silent feet, coming closer.

Slocum rolled to one side and plunged four feet down onto the Walapai brave. His elbow crashed into the brave's shoulder and knocked the man to his knees. Slocum's other arm whipped around the exposed neck and tightened. The brave struggled to get away, but Slocum's attack was too swift, too effective.

His knife came around and cut into the warrior's throat. But

Slocum stayed the deadly slash that would send a fountain of blood geysering forth.

He stared at his victim and a single word slipped from his lips.

"Charley!"

18

"Losing your nerve, Slocum?"

Slocum backed away, letting Walapai Charley go free. The Indian scout rubbed his neck where the knife had left a thin cut. Satisfied his throat had not been slit, Charley turned to face Slocum.

"I'm not going to kill you," Slocum said.

"Why not? I'm your enemy now. I left with Levy-Levy and joined Sherum."

Slocum shook his head. "I don't have a quarrel with you."

"That's good," Charley said.

Slocum froze when he heard movement behind him. Rifles cocked and he cast a quick glance over his shoulder. Three Walapai braves had him covered with their weapons, all stolen cavalry carbines. When Charley had left Camp Beale Springs he might have taken more than some jerky and beans with him.

"They won't kill you. You didn't kill me. Seems a fair trade. I certainly like it."

Slocum slid his knife into a sheath, wondering what to do now. He could never run for it without getting a dozen bullets in the back. Fighting free proved out of the question now that Walapai Charley had others backing him up.

"What do we do now?"

"I always liked talking. You think Captain Byrne would talk?"

Slocum laughed harshly. Byrne would do about anything to save his own neck and keep it intact for more liquor to flow down.

"This is Chief Levy-Levy," Charley said, lifting his head slightly and indicating a burly Indian holding a rifle leveled on Slocum. "He got fed up, too."

"Can't blame him. But it surprised me seeing you here. Did you plan the trap that got the cavalry?"

"Sherum," Charley said carefully, "is a very clever man. With fresh recruits from Levy-Levy's band, Sherum might be a problem for years to come. If Eastman had not tried to cheat the Walapai out of the promised land, Levy-Levy would still be content to struggle along with the half-rations."

"Eastman was shortchanging on the rations, just like McCue had done?"

"Yes," Charley said. This was nothing Slocum hadn't known, but he wanted Charley to confirm it. Eastman was as big a crook as McCue ever had been. And Gorman pulled the strings, though he could not prove the lieutenant masterminded the entire corrupt scheme.

"What will it take to get Levy-Levy back to the reservation?"

"No land along the Colorado River. Farming is for Mojaves. We are hunters. Give us land to hunt the deer." Charley snorted like a bull ready to paw the ground and charge. "Give us land with prairie dogs to hunt, if there's no deer. But no farming."

Sometimes Slocum could not tell when Charley was joking.

"And the supplies. We need the promised supplies to feed our people since the reservation does not extend as far as our original hunting lands."

"No meddling," Levy-Levy chimed in. "No meddling with our ways."

"The chief says to butt out," Charley explained, as if Slocum had not understood the plain words spoken in English. "Let us be. Let us solve our own problems without constant interference."

"This is all pretty much what the original treaty said, isn't it?" asked Slocum.

Charley nodded. Levy-Levy came over and whispered for some time to the scout. Charley's face never changed expression as the chief continued to speak. But of what? Slocum began to feel the hairs on the back of his neck rise. The other Walapais had not lowered their carbines. A slip on one trigger would send hot lead cutting through his back.

Finally, Levy-Levy finished his piece. Charley nodded again.

"Levy-Levy will not deal with Henry Eastman. He will talk again to Captain Byrne, if the man is sober. Before this pow-wow, Sherum must also agree to leave the warpath and take part."

"Levy-Levy wants me to convince Sherum to accept him as sole chief of the Walapai?" Slocum almost laughed at that.

"Never happen, Slocum," Charley said. "Levy-Levy won't leave the warpath unless Sherum does, too. But he can deal with Sherum himself, over who is to lead the tribe. Levy-Levy is sure the others will follow him if the treaty is honored."

"What do you want me to do?"

Charley looked quickly in Levy-Levy's direction, then back. He rubbed his chin and thought a while on it. Slocum grew nervous, wondering if Charley was preparing him for a bullet in the back. But the scout finally came to a decision.

"What Chief Levy-Levy wants is dangerous. He wants you to bring Sherum to the powwow."

"Me?"

"Sherum knows you. He admires your bravery," Charley said, smiling crookedly. "He thinks you are crazy to walk about with lighted sticks of dynamite, but he also respects your skill as a tracker. Never has a white eyes followed him so well."

"I've had your help."

"Sherum doesn't like me too much after I talked him into signing the last treaty. Nothing worked out right."

"You are his half brother. If you can't get him to palaver, how do I persuade him to parley again?" Slocum was at a loss to understand how to do this. Sherum had spent enough time on his own to learn to enjoy freedom. Being cooped up on a reservation, either around Beale Springs or along the Colorado River, was akin to imprisonment. Worse, the renegade chief had firsthand knowledge of how the cavalry dealt with Indians both on and off the reservation. Any sane man was likely to choose to die in battle rather than starve.

Dishonest men like Henry Eastman and John McCue—and Samuel Gorman—would always cause problems. Getting rid of them would improve the chances for peace in Arizona Territory. But Slocum knew he could do little to stop Gorman, short of shooting him down, and Henry Eastman lay beyond his ability to remove.

"I don't have your gift of gab," Slocum said. "We ought to get Dan Smith to help out. He's a smooth talker."

"We don't need smooth talkers," Charley said. "Too many of them have put us in this position."

"What will you do if I can't convince Sherum to lay down his rifle?"

"There won't be anyone returning to Camp Beale Springs," Charley said simply.

"That doesn't do you any good. Kill Byrne and the others, and more will come. There will be a constant blue tide of soldiers washing over Arizona until you are swept away. The Walapai won't even have a strip along the Colorado River to call their own."

"See?" said Charley. "You talk pretty good. Tell this to Sherum."

Slocum slumped under the weight of responsibility. He didn't want to be responsible for peace in the territory. He was a scout and a good one. The last time he had crossed Sherum's path, Sherum had been torturing Moira Kelson's brother to death and had not meant her any good, either. He had no kindly feelings toward the rebellious chief, but he had to admit he saw little to keep Sherum on a reservation.

"Nobody wins if you kill Byrne's troopers," Slocum said. "What happens if General Crook turns his attention to you from the Apaches down in Mexico? He's like the wind. You can never stop him."

"No one lives forever. Talk to Sherum. Do what is needed, and Byrne and the others might live to see another sunrise— and another bottle of whiskey."

"Where is Sherum?" Slocum asked, knowing he faced an impossible task.

There were far more warriors than Slocum anticipated. Sherum had rallied every stray Walapai in the Black Mountains to his war party. And half of them rose with weapons in hand when Levy-Levy, Charley, and Slocum walked into the camp.

Slocum looked straight ahead as he walked, trying to ignore the knives slashing close to his face and the lances cutting his clothing. To betray even an iota of fear now spelled his death.

"How'd I ever get myself into this?" he muttered when he saw Sherum again. The chief stared at him, and the look was dark and unfriendly.

Levy-Levy rattled on in Walapai for several minutes before sitting to one side. Charley remained at Slocum's side. In a low voice he said, "You're not too well received, but do your best."

"What happens to you and Levy-Levy if I fail?"

"Worry about your own scalp," Charley advised. "But if it makes you feel any better, we probably won't die until a week from next Tuesday. Sherum can be very inventive when he starts to torture."

"You dare come to my camp?" Chief Sherum walked forward. Slocum made a sudden move, as if throwing something to the chief. Sherum jumped back. A few braves laughed but were quickly silenced by Sherum's cold look. Slocum knew immediately who had been with Sherum near the Three Card Monte when they were torturing Monty Kelson.

"I would convince you there is another way of gaining your own land where you can hunt," Slocum said. "Killing the bluecoats will only bring you more misery."

"It will bring me satisfaction!"

"I'm sure," Slocum said, "but you are a great chief and a great chief has only his people's interests at heart. You would never give in to revenge if you can get land and food for all time."

"We are not like you. We fight. We do not talk our enemies to death."

"Slocum, that's a challenge," Charley whispered. "You don't have much choice. Accept it or die on the spot."

Slocum had already figured that out. He slowly unbuckled his gun belt and let it drop to the dirt. With deliberate moves, he drew his knife and held it in front of him, point aimed skyward.

"If I win, you will talk peace again with Captain Byrne. You need not agree to what he offers, but you will talk again."

"If you lose?" Sherum asked, drawing his own knife. The easy way he moved, the sharp tip gleaming in the low campfire light, the stark power locked with the chief's body all told Slocum he had to end the fight quickly. He could never overcome such a powerful and skillful warrior if the fight dragged on long.

"I die," Slocum said simply.

Sherum rushed forward, his blade driving up in a silvery arc intended to spit Slocum. But Slocum moved to the left, getting out of the way of the deadly upstroke. He jabbed and recovered, not intending to do much damage. He cut open Sherum's buckskin jacket but did not draw blood. The nearness of the blade was enough to turn Sherum more cautious. Only in slowing the man's attack could Slocum hope to win.

Circling, they feinted a few times, then Sherum charged. Slocum used his knife to block Sherum's thrust. Then they went down in a heap on the ground. Curling into a ball, Slocum got his feet up and shoved them hard into the Walapai chief's belly. Grabbing the chief's fringed buckskin jacket, Slocum pulled downward as he kicked up and rolled. Sherum cartwheeled above him, landing hard in the middle of the campfire.

Embers flew like crazed fireflies, and Sherum yelped as he beat out small fires on his clothing. His eyes widened as he again faced Slocum.

No blood had been drawn yet. Slocum knew he dared not toy with Sherum or one of them would die. Who won then? Sherum had promised to negotiate with Byrne. If the Walapai chief died, would Levy-Levy assume leadership and parley? Or was another of the hotheaded young bucks cheering their chief on likely to continue the rampage?

Sherum had to survive this fight. And Slocum wanted to come out alive, too.

Sherum danced forward, moving lightly. His knife shot forth like a striking rattler. Slocum winced as the knife tip raked the length of his forearm. Then he screamed in pain and dropped the knife.

For a split second, triumph flashed across Sherum's face. His eyes darted from Slocum to the dropped knife to the wounded arm. Then he realized how he had been duped.

Slocum had broken his concentration long enough to move to one side. As Sherum swung around, trying to slash open Slocum's belly, he found it was too late. Slocum moved behind him. A thick arm locked on his exposed throat and a knee drove hard into Sherum's spine, bending him backward.

As the Walapai chief tried to slash at Slocum's punishing arm, he found his wrist captured. Applying more pressure, Slocum bent the man double. The knife fell from Sherum's grip as Slocum twisted savagely on the wrist. But the forearm tightening on his throat and the knee in the back caused the chief the most distress.

He thrashed about, futilely trying to escape. His efforts grew weaker as his breath was cut off. Finally, Sherum slumped. Slocum was wary of any trick and maintained the pressure on the chief's windpipe for a few more seconds before lowering him to the ground.

Sherum gasped for air when Slocum released his punishing grip. He shoved Sherum forward, to fall on hands and knees. Grabbing his knife, Slocum held it high over his head for all to see. Then he drew back and let fly. The blade turned over and over and sank into the ground—inches from Sherum's hand.

"I could have killed you, Chief," Slocum gasped out. He fought to control his runaway heart. "I would rather you be talked to death by Captain Byrne. We *will* have peace. We will.''

Sherum dropped to a sitting position and grabbed the knife sunk into the ground. He pulled it free, his gaze hot with the fever of battle. As Slocum watched, that heat cooled. Sherum tossed the knife back.

"We will talk."

19

"We don't have to be at the land agent's office for an hour yet," Moira Kelson said as she looked up and down Prescott's main street.

"There's almost a festival atmosphere in town," Slocum said, noting the red, white, and blue banners and the way politicians gave speeches from the back of flatbed wagons. "It's hard to believe they're going to this trouble for the signing of another peace treaty, after the poor results on the last two."

"Peace," sighed Moira. "I wish something could have been done to that terrible Chief Sherum."

Slocum held his tongue. He had not told Moira how the peace conference had come about after he had bested Sherum in their fight. She would have wanted him to sink his knife all the way into the chief's back to garner some small measure of revenge for her brother's death. All he had said was that Captain Byrne had talked with Levy-Levy, and the two of them had convinced Sherum to come to terms.

Slocum got no credit for the peace treaty that was to be signed so publicly in an hour, and he wanted none.

"One good thing has come out of it, at least," Moira sighed. She brushed her flame-red hair back and stared at him with her emerald eyes. "The mining company's offer for the Three Card Monte is more than fair."

"Glad you accepted," Slocum said. "Finding another buyer might have taken a spell."

"You certainly deserve your fee," she said, turning suddenly shy.

"I won't get it till the company pays Joe Sanderson, and he takes his cut."

"That's not what I meant, John." She shyly tugged at his hand, and he let her pull him along toward her hotel. Being so close to the woman stirred Slocum's passions, and knowing she wanted him, too, added to the fire burning in his loins. She went up the steep hotel stairs ahead of him. He could hardly restrain himself. The movement of her bustle drove him wild.

Moira fumbled at the door. Slocum grabbed the key from her hand, shoved it into the lock and twisted savagely.

"You're taking too long," he said.

Moira spun about and threw her arms around his neck. She pulled him close and gave him a kiss hot enough to burn asbestos curtains. Her fingers stroked over his head, knocking his hat to the floor. He did not bother trying to pick it up. He was too busy returning the kiss.

When her tongue sneaked from between her ruby lips and entered his mouth, he knew he had to have her.

But again Moira was ahead of him.

Her fingers left his thick black hair and stroked over his strong arms and down to his slim hips. From there she worked around and got her hands on the buttoned fly holding him away from her.

"In the room," he urged. "Not here in the hall where someone might see us."

"I don't care!" she said hotly. "I want you. Now. Now, John, *now*!"

She got the last of the buttons free and let his steely hard manhood pop out. She caught it in the circle of her fingers and began stroking. Slocum tried to protest, then found words would not come. He closed his eyes and let the wondrous sensations rip into his body. His loins were on fire and it spread. Fast. Like a prairie fire.

He moved even closer and crushed her against the hallway wall. Moira moaned softly and widened her stance. Slocum grabbed double handfuls of her skirt and began lifting. It seemed to go on forever until Moira helped. She got some of the frilly undergarments out of their way, and Slocum found himself pressing against red-furred thatch nestled between her milky thighs.

"Yes, John, oh, yes," she sighed. She tossed her head back and then found no escape. He held her too firmly.

She reached between their bodies and caught his shaft. She guided it directly to the spot they both sought to have filled. Moira lifted one leg and hooked it around Slocum's waist, situating herself just right. The tip of Slocum's meaty spear sank into her moist inner fastness—then seemed to catch.

Moira gasped and did a little crow hop, like a horse trying to throw a rider. But she only positioned herself better. Both legs locked around his waist, she bounced up and down a few times until he slid balls deep into her quivering interior.

"You are so big," she sobbed, pressing her face into his neck. Slocum almost lost control then. She surrounded him totally. Her legs gripped him firmly. Her arms held him. And all around his throbbing length her most intimate flesh clutched like a hand in a soft velvet glove.

He kissed her swanlike neck and worked lower, holding her

off the floor. Turning a little, he let her drop away from the wall. Moira emitted a gasp of surprise, then followed it immediately with one of joy. His lips worked down her throat toward the deep canyon between her breasts. His tongue probed and darted, licking and leaving behind a hot trail of saliva. Every square inch of softly exposed skin he kissed until her passions rose to a furious pitch.

"Move, John, do it to me. I need to feel you moving in me," she gasped out.

Slocum's hands worked down her back until he cupped her sleek buttocks. He gripped those twin mounds of flesh and squeezed hard. Like kneading bread, he gave them his full attention. Then he lifted her a little, only to let her sink back. This movement carried her a few inches along his swollen staff. Using his grip, he moved her faster and faster until she was flying like a shuttlecock.

"John, wait, someone's coming!" Moira cried.

"I know," he said. "I know! It's you!"

"Wait, no, oh!"

He burned away any worry she might have had at being discovered in the hallway with his quick, sure movements. He began to burn like a miner's fuse. Inch by inch the heat spread down until his balls exploded in a fierce outpouring. Twisting and turning, gripping even harder on her fleshy buttocks, he gave her as much pleasure as he received.

Moira flopped hard against the wall and tried to lift herself by sheer will. With her legs so firmly locked around his waist, she could not escape—and she did not want to. She rode the winds of delight blowing through the hallway and finally sagged. He caught her before she collapsed onto the hallway floor.

"John, it was so good. I've never felt so, so—"

"I know," he said, gazing down at her. Slocum helped her stand. Then he buttoned himself up as she smoothed her skirts and tried to get her bodice decent again. He had pushed much of the cloth away from her breasts, leaving one to hang out delightfully. Moira tucked herself away chastely just as a gasping, harrumphing middle-aged man with walrus mustaches climbed the stairs.

He glared at them as he pushed past.

Moira had to laugh.

"What would he have said if he—?"

"It doesn't matter. You're not staying in Prescott after the mine is sold, are you?"

"Well, no I had thought to move on. I want to—" Moira was cut off by a loud shout from downstairs.

"Hey, Slocum, get your ass over to the courthouse. They're gettin' ready to sign the treaty, and Captain Byrne wants you there to watch. So does Chief Sherum." Corporal Framingham paused at the foot of the stairs, trying to figure why Slocum and Moira Kelson were laughing so. He shook his head and left. He had delivered the message.

"You can get your ass here anytime you want," Moira said seductively. She stood on tiptoe and nibbled at his ear. Then she said, "You had better go now. I'll see to the mine. Mr. Sanderson ought to have the money."

"All right," Slocum said, not wanting to go yet knowing he had to. He settled his gun belt around his middle, though he doubted he would be using the Colt slung so easily in the cross-draw holster. He stepped into the hot July sun beating down on Prescott and broke into a sweat.

Or was it he simply noticed the sweat he had built up while with Moira?

It had been a hell of a few months since the first treaty.

The ceremony was already under way when he went up the courthouse steps and ducked into the back of the crowded room.

"Chief Sherum now signs his name next to that of Chief

Levy-Levy and Captain Thomas Byrne,'' intoned Daniel Smith. The interpreter watched over Sherum's shoulder, then quickly witnessed the signature. "There is now officially peace between the people of Arizona Territory, the United States of America, and the Walapai nation!"

A cheer went up, but Captain Byrne lifted his hand to silence it.

"This is a great day, all parties agreeing to peaceful living, but there are a few things I need to do before the celebrating really starts," Byrne said. "First off, I checked the scales Mr. Eastman used to weigh out the rations given the Walapai."

Byrne signaled and two soldiers grabbed Eastman by the arms.

"Mr. Eastman is under arrest for theft. I reckon he stole close to five hundred pounds of beef and a thousand of beans and flour. He's not going to continue this practice."

"Wait," Sherum said. He spoke rapidly in Walapai. Smith interpreted.

"The chief asks who will be in charge of dispensing the rations."

"Sergeant Donnelly is a good man," Byrne said. "Is it satisfactory to the great chiefs that Donnelly be in charge?"

Sherum and Levy-Levy spoke quietly for a moment, then both nodded.

Slocum hitched his gun and shifted a little. Putting Eastman in jail was one thing. The real thief still stood behind Byrne. Lieutenant Gorman looked a mite peaked. He began edging toward the side door to the courthouse. Slocum ducked back into the blistering noonday heat and went around to the side in time to stop Gorman from mounting his horse.

"Going back to camp, Lieutenant?" Slocum asked.

"That's none of your business. I ought to—"

"Do what, Gorman? We both know who the thief is. I don't know or care if the loss of your family made you want to cheat the Walapai or if it's just pure cussedness on your part. You're not going to get away with what you've done.''

"You can't prove a thing. Byrne killed McCue. And Eastman is too scared ever to testify against me.''

"Who said anything about a trial?'' Slocum pointed. From the courthouse came a dozen Walapai warriors. Walapai Charley stood in front of the braves, hand on a feathered war lance. His fingers danced up and down the wooden length, ready to grip and throw. Sam Gorman would be dead in a flash.

"Don't,'' Slocum warned. The officer started to reach for the six-shooter holstered at his side. Slocum's stance showed he was ready to throw down on Gorman. The lieutenant didn't have a chance of getting the awkwardly holstered six-gun out before Slocum cut him down.

"What do you want from me?'' Gorman sweat blood now. His hand trembled, and he was only a step away from taking off and running. Three of the Walapai braves moved, nocked arrows, and stood waiting, as if wanting him to hightail it.

"They want your scalp. I want to get even for you sending McCue to ambush me. Fact is, you were out at the sulfur springs with him. I heard that big yellow dog of yours barking.''

"Ulysses,'' Walapai Charley said. "He barked because I was there.'' Hefting the lance, Charley balanced it easily. A flick of his wrist would pin Gorman to the courthouse wall.

"I won't let you do this to me, Slocum.''

"You can try to stop me,'' Slocum said. He hoped Gorman would reach for his pistol. Even the slightest movement would justify shooting the lieutenant. But Gorman realized that.

"I . . . I'm going back inside now. You can't stop me. There's a treaty.''

"Even in the middle of the night?'' asked Charley. "When no one's around but you? The dog might not give enough warning. Fact is, the dog's taken a liking to me.''

"Ulysses has not!"

"Can you count on that?" Slocum asked. "Charley's more patient than I am. You tried to shoot me in the back. I'll give you a fair chance to defend yourself before I shoot you. Unless—"

"Unless what?" Gorman's uniform clung to his body, soggy with sweat. "Unless what, Slocum?"

"You might confess to Captain Byrne what all's been going on at the camp. How you and McCue and Eastman were all in cahoots."

"He'd court-martial me!"

"Reckon so," Slocum said. "I'll just shoot you down like the mangy cayuse you are."

"I'd skin you alive, if my brothers didn't get to you first. Sherum has great ideas about torture. He enjoys it." Walapai Charley smiled, and it might have been the gates of hell opening.

Lieutenant Gorman swallowed hard and bolted back into the courthouse. Slocum heard the rush of confession to Thomas Byrne. If Byrne stayed sober long enough, he would bring the proper charges against Gorman.

Slocum touched the brim of his hat and walked away, leaving Charley and the other Walapai in silence. He didn't know if this was justice enough for the Indians. He hoped so. And if Gorman somehow escaped punishment in his court-martial, Slocum knew he would hear of it.

He could return to Prescott for such important unfinished business.

He stopped in front of the land agent's office in time to see Joe Sanderson counting out a stack of greenbacks onto his desk. Moira Kelson tucked them into her small purse and shook hands with the agent. Then she came out.

"John, there you are. I have your money, too. Mr. Sanderson gave it to me when I said I'd be seeing you." She reached into the small purse to withdraw the money. He grabbed her slender wrist, stopping her.

"Don't go flashing a wad of bills in public. The town's celebrating," Slocum said. "That doesn't mean there aren't desperados around willing to steal it."

"Oh, yes, of course, you are right," Moira said. She peered at him as if not knowing what to say. "When do you want your share? It's not much. Mr. Sanderson only got a thousand dollars for the claim. He kept one hundred as his share."

Slocum nodded. If he took another ten percent, that left Moira with eight hundred dollars. Not a great sum but enough to keep her going until something better turned up.

"I reckon we ought to decide where I'll collect it."

"Where?" An impish smile flickered on Moira's lips. "My room?"

"Maybe. Or perhaps in San Francisco. You mentioned wanting to see that town."

"Yes, I did. Perhaps you can show it to me. And collect your . . . due." Moira Kelson held out her arm and Slocum took it. San Francisco sounded just fine to her. And to him. From there he might drift on up the coast to Oregon as he had planned months earlier. Or simply go wherever the winds of chance blew him.

Until then, he would enjoy Moira's company. He could not ask for any more than that.

A special offer for people who enjoy reading the best Westerns published today.

WESTERNS!

NO OBLIGATION

Mail the coupon below

To start your subscription and receive 2 FREE WESTERNS, fill out the coupon below and mail it today. We'll send your first shipment which includes 2 FREE BOOKS as soon as we receive it.

Mail To: **True Value Home Subscription Services, Inc. P.O. Box 5235**
120 Brighton Road, Clifton, New Jersey 07015-5235

YES! I want to start reviewing the very best Westerns being published today. Send me my first shipment of 6 Westerns for me to preview FREE for 10 days. If I decide to keep them, I'll pay for just 4 of the books at the low subscriber price of $2.75 each; a total $11.00 (a $21.00 value). Then each month I'll receive the 6 newest and best Westerns to preview Free for 10 days. If I'm not satisfied I may return them within 10 days and owe nothing. Otherwise I'll be billed at the special low subscriber rate of $2.75 each; a total of $16.50 (at least a $21.00 value) and save $4.50 off the publishers price. There are never any shipping, handling or other hidden charges. I understand I am under no obligation to purchase any number of books and I can cancel my subscription at any time, no questions asked. In any case the 2 FREE books are mine to keep.

Name _____

Street Address _____ Apt. No. _____

City _____ State _____ Zip Code _____

Telephone _____

Signature _____
(if under 18 parent or guardian must sign)

Terms and prices subject to change. Orders subject
to acceptance by True Value Home Subscription
Services, Inc.

11924-5

JAKE LOGAN

TODAY'S HOTTEST ACTION WESTERN!